William Shakespeare's The Merry Wives of Windsor: A Retelling in Prose

David Bruce

Published by David Bruce, 2022.

This is a work of fiction. Similarities to real people, places, or events are entirely coincidental.

WILLIAM SHAKESPEARE'S THE MERRY WIVES OF WINDSOR: A RETELLING IN PROSE

First edition. July 27, 2022.

Copyright © 2022 David Bruce.

ISBN: 979-8201136871

Written by David Bruce.

Table of Contents

CAST OF CHARACTERS 1
CHAPTER 1 | — 1.1 — 3
— 1.2 — 17
— 1.3 — 18
— 1.4 — 24
CHAPTER 2 | — 2.1 — 30
— 2.2 — 39
— 2.3 — 49
CHAPTER 3 | — 3.1 — 54
— 3.2 — 59
— 3.3 — 63
— 3.4 — 71
— 3.5 — 75
CHAPTER 4 | — 4.1 — 80
— 4.2 — 85
— 4.3 — 92
— 4.4 — 93
— 4.5 — 96
— 4.6 — 101
CHAPTER 5 | — 5.1 — 103
— 5.2 — 105
— 5.3 — 106
— 5.4 — 107
— 5.5 — 108
APPENDIX A: ABOUT THE AUTHOR 118
APPENDIX B: SOME BOOKS BY DAVID BRUCE 119

Dedication

Dedicated to Carl Eugene Bruce and Josephine Saturday Bruce

My father, Carl Eugene Bruce, died on 24 October 2013. He used to work for Ohio Power, and at one time, his job was to shut off the electricity of people who had not paid their bills. He sometimes would find a home with an impoverished mother and some children. Instead of shutting off their electricity, he would tell the mother that she needed to pay her bill or soon her electricity would be shut off. He would write on a form that no one was home when he stopped by because if no one was home he did not have to shut off their electricity.

The best good deed that anyone ever did for my father occurred after a storm that knocked down many power lines. He and other linemen worked long hours and got wet and cold. Their feet were freezing because water got into their boots and soaked their socks. Fortunately, a kind woman gave my father and the other linemen dry socks to wear.

My mother, Josephine Saturday Bruce, died on 14 June 2003. She used to work at a store that sold clothing. One day, an impoverished mother with a baby clothed in rags walked into the store and started shoplifting in an interesting way: The mother took the rags off her baby and dressed the infant in new clothing. My mother knew that this mother could not afford to buy the clothing, but she helped the mother dress her baby and then she watched as the mother walked out of the store without paying.

***

The doing of good deeds is important. As a free person, you can choose to live your life as a good person or as a bad person. To be a good person, do good deeds. To be a bad person, do bad deeds. If you do good deeds, you will become good. If you do bad deeds, you will become bad. To become the person you want to be, act as if you already are that kind of person. Each of us chooses what kind of person we will become. To become a good person, do the things a good person does. To become a bad person, do the things a bad person does. The opportunity to take action to become the kind of person you want to be is yours.

Human beings have free will. According to the Babylonian Niddah 16b, whenever a baby is to be conceived, the Lailah (angel in charge of contraception) takes the drop of semen that will result in the conception and asks God, "Sovereign of the Universe, what is going to be the fate of this drop? Will it develop into a robust or into a weak person? An intelligent or a stupid person? A wealthy or a poor person?" The Lailah asks all these questions, but it does not ask, "Will it develop into a righteous or a wicked person?" The answer to that question lies in the decisions to be freely made by the human being that is the result of the conception.

A Buddhist monk visiting a class wrote this on the chalkboard: "EVERYONE WANTS TO SAVE THE WORLD, BUT NO ONE WANTS TO HELP MOM DO THE DISHES." The students laughed, but the monk then said, "Statistically, it's highly unlikely that any of you will ever have the opportunity to run into a burning orphanage and rescue an infant. But, in the smallest gesture of kindness — a warm smile, holding the door for the person behind you, shoveling the driveway of the elderly person next door — you have committed an act of immeasurable profundity, because to each of us, our life is our universe."

In her book titled *I Have Chosen to Stay and Fight*, comedian Margaret Cho writes, "I believe that we get complimentary snack-size portions of the afterlife, and we all receive them in a different way." For Ms. Cho, many of her snack-size portions of the afterlife come in hip hop music. Other people get different snack-size portions of the afterlife, and we all must be on the lookout for them when they come our way. And perhaps doing good deeds and experiencing good deeds are snack-size portions of the afterlife.

The Zen master Gisan was taking a bath. The water was too hot, so he asked a student to add some cold water to the bath. The student brought a bucket of cold water, added some cold water to the bath, and then threw the rest of the water on a rocky path. Gisan scolded the student: "Everything can be used. Why did you waste the rest of the water by pouring it on the path? There are some plants nearby which could have used the water. What right do you have to waste even a drop of water?" The student became enlightened and changed his name to Tekisui, which means "Drop of Water."

Educate Yourself
Read Like A Wolf Eats
Be Excellent to Each Other
Books Then, Books Now, Books Forever

***

In this retelling, as in all my retellings, I have tried to make the work of literature accessible to modern readers who may lack some of the knowledge about mythology, religion, and history that the literary work's contemporary audience had.

Do you know a language other than English? If you do, I give you permission to translate this book, copyright your translation, publish or self-publish it, and keep all the royalties for yourself. (Do give me credit, of course, for the original retelling.)

I would like to see my retellings of classic literature used in schools, so I give permission to the country of Finland (and all other countries) to give copies of this book to all students forever. I also give permission to the state of Texas (and all other states) to give copies of this book to all students forever. I also give permission to all teachers to give copies of this book to all students forever.

Teachers need not actually teach my retellings. Teachers are welcome to give students copies of my eBooks as background material. For example, if they are teaching Homer's *Iliad* and *Odyssey*, teachers are welcome to give students copies of my *Virgil's* Aeneid: *A Retelling in Prose* and tell students, "Here's another ancient epic you may want to read in your spare time."

CAST OF CHARACTERS

Male Characters

SIR JOHN FALSTAFF.

MR. FENTON, a young Gentleman, in love with Anne Page.

ROBERT SHALLOW, a Country Justice.

ABRAHAM SLENDER, Nephew to Justice Shallow.

FRANK FORD: a Gentleman dwelling at Windsor.

GEORGE PAGE: a Gentleman dwelling at Windsor.

WILLIAM PAGE, a Boy, Son to Page.

SIR HUGH EVANS, a heavily accented Welsh Parson.

DOCTOR CAIUS, a heavily accented French Physician.

HOST of the Garter Inn.

BARDOLPH, PISTOL, and NYM: Followers (attendants) of Falstaff.

ROBIN, Page to Falstaff.

PETER SIMPLE, Servant to Slender.

JOHN RUGBY, Servant to Doctor Caius.

Female Characters

MRS. ALICE FORD, a merry wife.

MRS. MEG PAGE, a merry wife.

ANNE PAGE, her Daughter, in love with Fenton. Anne is sometimes called "Nan."

MISTRESS QUICKLY, Servant to Doctor Caius.

Minor Characters

Servants to Page, Ford, etc.

Scene

Windsor; and the Neighborhood. This play is set entirely in England.

Notes

• The comic Welsh accent of Sir Hugh Evans has these characteristics:

1) Sir Hugh often pronounces an initial *p* instead of *b*. E.g. *py = by, putter =butter*.

2) Sir Hugh often pronounces *f* instead of *v*. E.g. *fery = very*.

3) Sir Hugh often pronounces *t* instead of *d*. E.g. *goot = good, Got = God, worts = words*.

4) Sir Hugh often does not pronounce an initial *w*. E.g. *'oman = woman, 'orld = world, 'ork = work.*

5) Sir Hugh often misuses words; for example, he often uses a noun where an adjective ought to be used.

6) Sir Hugh often makes words plural when they should be singular.

• The comic French accent of Doctor Caius has these characteristics:

1) Doctor Caius often pronounces *d* or *t* instead of *th*. E.g. *dat = that, de = the,* troat = throat.

2) Doctor Caius often pronounces *v* instead of *w*, *wh*, or *f*. E.g. *vorld = world, vat = what, vetch = fetch.*

3) Doctor Caius often pronounces *p* instead of *b*. E.g. *Pible = Bible.*

4) Doctor Caius often does not pronounce an initial *g*. E.g. *'od's – God's.*

5) Doctor Caius often adds *a* to the end of a word. E.g. *Peace-a, speak-a.*

CHAPTER 1

— 1.1 —

In front of George Page's house in Windsor, three men were speaking: Robert Shallow, a Justice of the Peace; Abraham Slender, his nephew; and Sir Hugh Evans, a heavily accented Welsh parson. Sir Hugh was not a knight. He was entitled to use "Sir" in front of his name because he had received a university degree.

Justice Shallow said, "Sir Hugh, don't try to change my mind; I will make a Star Chamber matter of it: Even if he were twenty Sir John Falstaffs, he shall not abuse Robert Shallow, esquire."

Justice Shallow felt wronged by Sir John Falstaff and wanted to take him before the Star Chamber, a high court whose meeting place was in a chamber in the palace of Westminster. It was called the Star Chamber because the meeting room ceiling was decorated with stars. This court dealt with cases involving riotous behavior by men with titles.

Sir John Falstaff was a man with a title; he was a knight. Justice Shallow was an esquire, which is the rank immediately beneath the rank of knight.

Slender added more information about Justice Shallow's titles: "You are Robert Shallow, esquire in the county of Gloucester, justice of peace, and 'Coram.'"

By "Coram," Slender meant the Latin *quorum*, which was part of the formula for the installation of justices: *quorum vos ... unum esse volumus*, or "of whom we wish that you ... be one."

"Yes, cousin Slender," Justice Shallow said, "and 'Custalorum.'"

By "Custalorum," Justice Shallow meant the Latin *Custos Rotolurum*, which meant "Keeper of the Rolls," aka the Chief Justice of the Peace of the County.

Slender, who knew very little Latin, said, "Yes, and 'Ratolorum,' too."

He did not know that "Custalorum" and "Ratolorum" meant the same thing.

He said to Sir Hugh, "And Justice Shallow is a gentleman born, Master Parson; he writes 'Armigero' to describe himself in any bill, warrant, quittance, or obligation — 'Armigero.'"

By "Armigero," Slender meant *armiger*, which means "esquire" in Latin. Esquires were entitled to have a coat of arms.

"Yes, I do write myself 'esquire,'" Justice Shallow said, "and I have done that anytime these three hundred years."

He meant that he came from a long line of ancestors who were esquires.

"All his successors who have gone before him have done that, and all his ancestors who come after him will also do that," Slender said. "They may display the dozen white luces in their coat."

Slender referred to a coat of arms with a dozen white luces — the freshwater fish named pikes — on it. Often, he made mistakes; here, he had mixed up "ancestors" and "successors."

Justice Shallow said about his family's coat of arms, "It is an old coat."

Sir Hugh Evans, misunderstanding their conversation, said, "The dozen white louses do become an old coat well; it agrees well, passant; it is a familiar beast to man, and signifies love."

At the time, lice often infested old clothing, and at the time, lice were familiar to man. By "well, passant," Sir Hugh meant "passing well" or "very well," but *passant* is an Old French heraldic term meaning "walking." Anyone listening to Sir Hugh could think that he was talking about walking fish. Lice can signify love: Lice cling to men and never willingly separate themselves from men. Fish can also signify love; a fish was a symbol of Christianity, whose followers are supposed to be identified by their love.

Justice Shallow said, "The luce is the fresh fish."

He was letting Sir Hugh know that they were talking about freshwater fish, not about lice.

He added, "The salt fish is suitable for an old coat."

Salted fish are preserved fish that are meant to last for a long time; old coats of arms have lasted for a long time.

Slender said to his uncle, Justice Shallow, "I may quarter, kinsman."

By "quarter," he meant that it was possible for him to combine two coats of arms.

Justice Shallow replied, "You may, by marrying."

If Slender were to marry a woman from a family who had a coat of arms, he could combine the two coats of arms. The coat of arms would have four quarters, and in two quarters would appear his coat of arms while in the other two quarters would appear his wife's coat of arms.

Sir Hugh Evans misunderstood again and said, "It is marring indeed, if he quarter it."

He thought that they were talking about the garment of winter clothing known as a coat.

"Not at all," Justice Shallow said.

With his heavy Welsh accent, Sir Hugh said, "Yes, py'r [by our] lady; if he has a quarter of your coat, there is but three skirts for yourself, in my simple conjectures, but that is all one."

If a coat were torn into quarters, it would mar the coat. Some coats have four skirts, or sections: two in back, and two in front. If someone were to take a quarter of the coat, aka one skirt, only three skirts would be left in the marred coat.

Sir Hugh added, "If Sir John Falstaff has committed disparagements unto you, I am of the church, and will be glad to do my benevolence to make atonements and compremises [compromises] between you."

Sir Hugh was a good man who wanted to make peace between Justice Shallow and Sir John Falstaff, if possible.

"The council shall hear it," Justice Shallow said. "It is a case involving riotous behavior by a knight."

Sir Hugh misunderstood Justice Shallow. He thought that the word "council" referred to a church council, not to the Star Chamber.

Sir Hugh said, "It is not meet [fitting that] the council hear a riot; there is no fear of Got [God] in a riot; the council, look you, shall desire to hear the fear of Got, and not to hear a riot; take your vizaments [advisements] in that."

He wanted Justice Shallow to think carefully about his — Sir Hugh's — words.

"I swear on my life, if I were young again, the sword should end this disagreement," Justice Shallow said. "Sir John and I would fight."

"It is petter [better] that friends is the sword, and end it," Sir Hugh said.

This was good advice from a clergyman. Let friends — such as Sir Hugh — not swords, bring about peace.

Sir Hugh added, "There is also another device in my prain [brain], which peradventure prings goot [perhaps brings good] discretions with it: There is Anne Page, who is the daughter to Mr. George Page, who is pretty virginity."

By "goot discretions," Sir Hugh meant "a good suggestion" — he often used the plural when he should have used the singular. Unfortunately, through misplacing words, he had made "pretty virginity" refer to George Page, not to Anne Page. Sir Hugh should have placed the related words close together.

"Anne Page?" Slender asked. "Is she the one who has brown hair, and speaks in a low, delicate voice like a woman?"

"It is that fery [very] person for all the 'orld [world], as just as you will desire," Sir Hugh said, "Seven hundred pounds of moneys, and gold and silver, is her grandsire upon his death's-bed — may Got [God] deliver him to a joyful resurrections! — give to her when she is able to overtake seventeen years old."

In other words, when Anne Page is seventeen years old, she will inherit a considerable amount of money from her grandfather, who is now on his deathbed.

Sir Hugh continued, "It were a goot motion [good thing to do] if we leave our pribbles and prabbles [bribbles, aka quibbles, and brabbles, aka trivial disputes], and desire a marriage between Mr. Abraham Slender and Miss Anne Page."

"Did her grandfather leave her seven hundred pounds?" Slender, who was not in love with Anne Page, asked.

"Yes," Sir Hugh said, "and her father is make her a petter [better] penny."

Not only was Anne Page going to inherit much wealth from her grandfather, but her father would also give her a pretty penny.

"I know the young gentlewoman," Slender said. "She has good gifts."

By "good gifts," he meant "good characteristics and virtues."

Sir Hugh said, "Seven hundred pounds and possibilities [and possibly more money] is goot [good] gifts."

"Well, let us go and see good Mr. Page," Slender said. "Is Falstaff there at Mr. Page's house?"

"Shall I tell you a lie?" Sir Hugh said. "I do despise a liar as I do despise one who is false, or as I despise one who is not true. The knight, Sir John, is there; and, I beg you to be ruled by your well-willers [well-wishers]. I will peat [beat, aka knock on] the door for Mr. Page."

He knocked on the door and called, "Hello! Got pless [God bless] your house here!"

From inside his house, Mr. Page called, "Who's there?"

He opened his door.

Sir Hugh said, "Here is Got's plessing [God's blessing], and your friend, and Justice Shallow; and here is young Mr. Slender, that peradventures shall tell you another tale [perhaps will have something to tell you], if matters grow to your likings [if you are willing]."

Mr. Page said, "I am glad to see that all of you are well."

He added, "I thank you for the gift of venison you sent to me, Justice Shallow."

"Mr. Page, I am glad to see you," Justice Shallow said. "I wish you good health. I wish that the venison I sent to you were better; it was not killed in the best way for the meat to be at its tastiest. How is good Miss Page? I thank you always with my heart — with all my heart."

"Sir, I thank you," Mr. Page said.

"Sir, I thank you," Justice Shallow said. "By yea and no, I do."

Mr. Page said, "I am glad to see you, good Mr. Slender."

"How is your fawn-colored greyhound, sir?" Slender asked. "I heard it said that he was outrun in a race held at Cotsall."

Cotsall was a way of referring to the Cotswold Hills in Gloucestershire.

"It was too close to call, sir," Mr. Page said.

Slender teased him: "You won't admit that your dog was outrun."

"And he should not," Justice Shallow said. "You are at fault for teasing Mr. Page."

He added, "Mr. Page's dog is a good dog."

"My dog is a cur — an ordinary dog — sir," Mr. Page said.

"Sir, he's a good dog, and he is a fair dog," Justice Shallow said. "Can there be anymore said? He is both good and fair."

Justice Shallow added, "Is Sir John Falstaff here?"

"Sir, he is inside," Mr. Page said, "and I wish I could do a good turn for the two of you."

Sir Hugh said, "That is spoken as a Christians ought to speak."

"He has wronged me, Mr. Page," Justice Shallow said.

"Sir, he docs somewhat confess it," Mr. Page replied.

"Even if it is confessed, it is still not yet redressed," Justice Shallow said. "Is not that so, Master Page? He has wronged me; indeed he has, in a word — he has, believe me. I, Robert Shallow, esquire, say that I have been wronged."

"Here comes Sir John," Mr. Page said.

Sir John Falstaff and his followers Bardolph, Nym, and Pistol exited Mr. Page's house. Bardolph's face was red from his alcoholism, Nym's favorite word was "humor," and Pistol loved extravagant language of the type he heard in action-filled plays.

Falstaff, who knew that Justice Shallow was upset at him, said, "Justice Shallow, do you plan to complain about me to the King?"

Justice Shallow laid out the charges against Falstaff: "Knight, you have beaten my men, killed my deer, and broken open my lodge."

His lodge was his gamekeeper's dwelling in his park.

Falstaff asked, "Have I kissed your gamekeeper's daughter?"

"Tut, I don't care a pin about that trifling thing," Justice Shallow said. "These charges shall be answered."

He meant "answered in a court of law."

Falstaff, deliberately misunderstanding "answered" as "replied to," said, "I will answer it immediately; I have done everything that you have accused me of doing. That is now answered."

"The council shall know about this," Justice Shallow said.

"It would be better for you if it were known in counsel — that is privately," Falstaff replied. "If it is known publicly, you'll be laughed at."

"*Pauca verba*, Sir John," Sir Hugh said.

Pauca verba is Latin for "few words."

Sir Hugh added, "Goot worts [Good words]."

Worts are cabbage-like plants.

Pretending that Sir Hugh had meant to say "worts" instead of "words," Falstaff replied, "Good worts! Good cabbage."

He then said to Justice Shallow's nephew, "Slender, I broke your head and made it bleed. What matter have you against me?"

Falstaff meant "legal matter."

"Sir, I have matter in my head against you," Mr. Slender said, referring to his brain matter.

He added, "And I have matter against your cony-catching rascals: Bardolph, Nym, and Pistol."

Bardolph, Nym, and Pistol were all lowlife thieves and conmen. A cony is a rabbit, and "cony" is also a word for the victim of a con.

Slender continued, "They carried me to the tavern and made me drunk, and afterward they picked my pocket."

Drawing his sword, Bardolph called Slender a name: "You Banbury cheese!"

Banbury cheeses are made in thin rounds, and so they are a byword — an outstanding embodiment or example — for anything very thin.

Intimidated by Bardolph, Slender said, "Never mind. It does not matter."

"What is the meaning of this, Mephostophilus?" Pistol shouted as he drew his sword.

By "Mephostophilus," Pistol meant "Mephistophilis," a Devil who tempted Doctor Faustus in Christopher Marlowe's play *Doctor Faustus*.

Intimidated by Pistol, Slender said, "Never mind. It does not matter."

"Slice, I say!" Nym shouted as he drew his sword and made slicing motions with it. "*Pauca, pauca*! Slice! That's my humor. That's what I think."

Pauca is Latin for "few," and Pistol probably meant *Pauca verba*, aka "Few words." In other words, Pistol was saying, "Let's stop talking and instead start fighting!"

Intimidated by Nym, Slender asked, "Where is Peter Simple, my manservant? Can you tell me, uncle?"

He wanted someone to protect him from Falstaff's followers.

"Be quiet, please," Sir Hugh said. "Now let us understand this matter. There is three umpires in this matter, as I understand; that is, Master Page, *fidelicet* [*videlicet*, Latin for "namely"] Master Page; and there is myself, *fidelicet* myself; and the three [third] party is, lastly and finally, my Host of the Garter Inn."

"We three, then, are to hear it and end it between them," Mr. Page said. "We will hear about and judge the quarrel concerning Slender."

"Fery goot [Very good]," Sir Hugh said. "I will make a prief [brief] of it in my notebook; and we will afterwards 'ork [work] upon the cause with as great discreetly [discretion] as we can."

Falstaff acted as a lawyer in this mock trial. He called, "Pistol!"

"He hears with ears," Pistol replied.

"The tevil [Devil] and his tam [dam, aka mother]!" Sir Hugh said. "What phrase is this, 'He hears with ears'? Why, it is affectations [affected]!"

Falstaff asked, "Pistol, did you pick Mr. Slender's pocket?"

Slender said, "Yes, by these gloves, did he, or I wish that I might never come in my own great chamber — the largest room in my house — again otherwise. He robbed me of seven groats in mill-sixpences, and two Edward shovel-boards that cost me two shilling and two pence apiece when I bought them from Ed Miller, by these gloves."

A groat is a coin worth fourpence. A mill-sixpence is a sixpence that is made by a machine rather than made by hand. Because it is made by a machine, its edges are smoother and more regular than a sixpence made by hand. An Edward shovelboard is a shilling from the reign of King Edward VI; it was used as a counter in the game of shovelboard.

Falstaff asked, "Is this true, Pistol?"

Sir Hugh misunderstood Falstaff's words. He thought that Falstaff was referring to "true Pistol," aka "honest Pistol."

Sir Hugh said, "No; he is false Pistol, if he is a pickpocket."

"Ha, you mountain-foreigner!" Pistol said, referring to Sir Hugh's Welsh ancestry — Wales is known for its mountains. "Sir John and Justice Shallow, I combat challenge of this latten bilbo."

Pistol was saying that he wanted to fight Slender in a trial by combat. He insultingly called Slender a latten Bilbo — a brass sword. Iron swords are better than brass swords because iron is harder than brass. He was also comparing Slender's thinness to a skinny sword.

Pistol continued, "Word of denial in thy labras here! Word of denial: froth and scum, you lie!"

By "labras," Pistol meant "lips." He was saying that Slender was lying through his lips, and that he, Pistol, was forcing those lying words back into Slender's mouth. However, Pistol's Latin was poor. *Labrum* is Latin for lip; *labra* is the plural form. Both "froth and scum" refer to beer; the "scum" is the dregs of the beer, while froth is air bubbles mixed with beer. Pistol was insulting Slender by calling him froth and scum.

Intimidated by Pistol, Slender said, "By these gloves, if Pistol did not rob me, then it was he." He pointed at Nym.

Nym said, "Be advised, sir, and pass good humors — think carefully, and say good things about me."

He added, "I will say 'marry trap' with you, if you run the nuthook's humor on me; that is the very note of it."

Even at the best of times, Nym's language was difficult to understand. Possibly, he was using "trap" in its slang sense of "fraud" and was threatening to find out something bad about Slender and reveal it publicly. That is, he would marry, or join, the word "fraud" to Slender's name so that "Slender" would become synonymous with "fraud." A nutfork is a forked stick used to hook the branches of nut trees and pull them closer to the ground so that the nuts could be harvested. Police officers were called "nuthooks" because they would "hook" and arrest criminals.

Therefore, this is probably what Nym was saying: "If you try to get me arrested, I will dig up dirt on you and make your name synonymous with the word 'fraud' — I mean it."

Intimidated by Nym, Slender said, "By this hat, then, he in the red face — Bardolph — robbed me; for though I cannot remember what I did when you made me drunk, yet I am not altogether an ass."

Falstaff asked Bardolph, "What do you say, Scarlet and John?"

Slender had referred to Bardolph as "he in the red face" — cosmetics were regarded as a kind of mask, and Bardolph's face, which was red because of his alcoholism, looked as if a red color had been applied with a liberal use of cosmetics. Falstaff called Bardolph "Scarlet and John" as a reference to two of Robin Hood's companions: Will Scarlet and Little John. "Scarlet" was a reference to Bardolph's red face, or mask, and "John" was perhaps a reference to the person wearing the "mask." In folklore, Little John was a giant of a man, and so perhaps Bardolph has a beer belly — although not nearly as big as Falstaff's.

"Why, sir," Bardolph said, "for my part I say the gentleman had drunk himself out of his five sentences."

Sir Hugh said, "It is his five senses, not 'five sentences' — what the ignorance is!"

"And being fap, aka drunk, sir," Bardolph continued, "he was, as they say, cashiered — thrown out of the tavern — and so conclusions passed the careiers."

A careier, aka career, in horsemanship is a short run at full speed. Bardolph was saying that things swiftly came to their conclusions. He did not say what those conclusions were; he was hoping that the "umpires" would decide that the drunken Slender had lost his money instead of being robbed of it.

If you have trouble understanding Bardolph's words, you are not the only one. Slender actually thought that Bardolph was speaking a language other than English!

Slender said, "Yes, you spoke in Latin in the inn, too, as well as now, but it does not matter: I'll never be drunk again as long as I live, except in the company of honest, civil, godly people, as a result of this trick. If I am ever again drunk, I'll be drunk with those who have the fear of God, and not with drunken knaves."

"So Got 'udge [God judge] me," Sir Hugh said, "That is a virtuous mind."

Falstaff said, "You have heard all these matters denied, gentlemen; you have heard it."

Anne Page now arrived, carrying wine. Mrs. Ford and Mrs. Page followed her.

Mr. Page said, "No, daughter, carry the wine inside; we'll drink it inside the house."

Anne Page carried the wine back inside the house.

Slender said to himself, "Heaven! This is Miss Anne Page!"

"How are you, Mrs. Ford?" Mr. Page said.

"Mrs. Ford," Falstaff said, "truly it is good to see you again."

He added, "With your permission, good woman," and kissed her politely in greeting.

Mr. Page said to his wife, "Make these gentlemen welcome."

He said to the others, "Come, we are having a hot venison meat pie for dinner."

He wanted everyone to make peace with each other: Justice Shallow to make peace with Falstaff, and Slender to make peace with Pistol, Nym, and Bardolph. Therefore, he added, "Come, gentlemen, I hope we shall drink down all unkindness with our wine. Let all of us be at peace with each other."

Everyone went inside the Pages' house except for Justice Shallow, Slender, and Sir Hugh Evans.

Slender said, "I wish that I had my *Book of Songs and Sonnets* here. I would rather have that than forty shillings."

Simple, Slender's manservant, arrived.

Slender said, "How are you, Simple! Where have you been? I must wait on myself, must I? Do you have the *Book of Riddles* with you?"

"*Book of Riddles*!" Simple said. "Why, didn't you lend it to Alice Shortcake last Allhallowmas, a fortnight before Michaelmas?"

Allhallowmas is All Saints' Day: November 1. Michaelmas is Saint Michael's Day: September 29. Simple had made a mistake. He meant "Martlemas," not Michaelmas. Martlemas is November 11.

Justice Shallow said to Slender, "Come, let's go inside. We are waiting for you. But first let us have a word with you. Pay attention. There is, as it were, a tender, a kind of tender, made afar off — indirectly — by Sir Hugh here. Do you understand me?"

Slender said, "Yes, sir, you shall find me reasonable; if it be so, I shall do what is reasonable."

Slender thought he understood what tender had been made, but he did not. Justice Shallow was saying that Sir Hugh had indirectly stated that Slender was interested in marrying Anne Page; however, Slender thought that the tender referred to a reconciliation between himself and Falstaff's men: Pistol, Nym, and Bardolph.

"You don't understand me," Justice Shallow said.

"I do understand you, sir," Shallow replied.

"Give ear [Listen] to his motions [suggestions], Mr. Slender," Sir Hugh said. "I will description [describe] the matter to you, if you be capacity of it [are capable of understanding it]."

"No, I will do as my kinsman Justice Shallow says," Slender said, still thinking that they were talking about his dispute with Falstaff's men. "Please, pardon me; I will listen to him because he's a justice of peace in his country. I may be a simple man, but I know enough to listen to his advice about legal matters."

Sir Hugh said, "But that is not what we are talking about: We are not talking about legal matters. The matter we are talking about concerns your marriage."

"I see," Slender said.

"Yes," Sir Hugh said. "We are talking about you marrying Miss Anne Page."

"Why, if it must be so," Slender said, "I will marry her upon any reasonable demands."

"But can you affection [feel affection for; that is, love] the 'oman [woman]?" Sir Hugh asked. "Let us command [demand] to know that from your mouth or from your lips; for divers [several, diverse] philosophers hold that the lips is parcel [part] of the mouth. Therefore, precisely [concisely], can you carry your good will to the maiden?"

At the time, "will" could mean sexual desire; it could also mean genitals.

Justice Shallow asked, "Abraham Slender, can you love her?"

"I hope, sir," Slender replied, "that I will do as it shall become one who would do what is reasonable."

"Got's lords and His ladies!" Sir Hugh said. "You must speak possitable [positively and more passionately], if you can carry her your desires towards her [if you want to convince her that you love her]."

"Yes, you must do that," Justice Shallow said. "Will you, if she has a good dowry, marry her?"

"I will do a greater thing than that," Slender said, "upon your request, Justice Shallow, in any reasonable thing."

"Listen to me. Listen to me, sweet kinsman," Justice Shallow said. "What I am doing is meant to make you happy, Slender. Can you love the maiden?"

"I will marry her, sir, at your request," Slender replied, "but if there is no great love in the beginning, yet Heaven may decrease it upon better acquaintance, when we are married and have more occasion to know one another; I hope, upon familiarity will grow more contempt. But if you say, 'Marry her,' I will marry her; to do that I am freely dissolved, and dissolutely."

Slender lacked facility with language — Bardolph may have been correct when he said that Slender had drunk himself out of his five sentences. Slender had meant to say "increase," not "decrease"; "content," not "contempt"; "resolved," not "dissolved"; and "resolutely," not "dissolutely."

Sir Hugh said, "It is a fery discretion [very discrete, by which Sir Hugh meant "very good"] answer, except for the mistake in the 'ort [word] 'dissolutely': The 'ort is, according to our meaning, 'resolutely,' but Slender's meaning — his content — is good."

"Yes, I think my nephew Slender meant well," Justice Shallow said.

"Yes, or else I wish that I might be hanged!" Slender said.

"Here comes fair — beautiful — Miss Anne," Justice Shallow said.

He said to her, "I wish that I were young again because of you, Miss Anne!"

Anne Page replied politely, "The dinner is on the table; my father desires your company."

Justice Shallow said, "I will go in and eat with him, beautiful Miss Anne."

"'od's plessed [God's blessed] will!" Sir Hugh said. "I will not be absence [absent] at the grace."

Justice Shallow and Sir Hugh went inside.

Anne Page asked Slender, "Will you please come in and eat, sir?"

"No, thank you," Slender replied. "I thank you, heartily. I am very well."

"The people inside are waiting for you, sir," Anne Page said.

"I am not hungry, thank you," Slender said.

He said to his manservant Simple, "Go inside. Although you are my manservant, you can wait upon my uncle, Justice Shallow."

Simple went inside.

Slender said, "A justice of peace sometimes may be beholden to his friend for the use of a manservant. I have only three men and a boy as my servants, until my mother dies and leaves me an inheritance, but so what? It does not matter that I am living as if I were born a poor gentleman."

"I may not go in without you," Anne Page said. "They will not sit at the table and eat until you come."

If Slender were intelligent, he would know that he ought to go inside immediately. He was not intelligent.

"Truly, I'll eat nothing," he said. "I thank you as much as though I did eat."

"Please, sir, go inside."

"I had rather walk here, outside, I thank you," Slender said. "I bruised my shin the other day with playing at sword and dagger with a master of fence; we fought three bouts for a dish of stewed prunes; and, truly, I cannot abide the smell of hot meat since."

Slender had no idea how to court a woman — or how to fence. He must have stumbled and bruised his shin while fencing, and he ought to have known that "stewed prunes" was a way of referring to a prostitute — stewed prunes were served in brothels. He was giving Anne Page the impression that he had injured himself while fighting over a whore. He also should have known that the phrase "hot meat" had a secondary meaning of "prostitute."

Dogs had been barking, and Slender asked Anne Page, "Why do your dogs bark so? Are there bears in the town?"

Bears were used in the "sport" of bearbaiting. A bear would be tied to a stake, and then dogs would be let loose to attack the bear.

"I think there are, sir," Anne Page said. "I heard them being talked about."

"I love the sport well, but I shall as quickly quarrel with another spectator at a bearbaiting as any man in England," Slender said. "You would be afraid, if you were to see a bear loose, wouldn't you?"

"Yes, indeed, sir," she replied.

"That's meat and drink to me, now. I have seen the famous bear Sackerson loose twenty times, and I have taken him by the chain," Slender said, "but, I promise you, the women have so cried and shrieked at it, that it surpassed all belief, but women, indeed, cannot abide bears; they are very ill-favored — ugly — and rough things."

Presumably, Slender was calling the bears — not the women — ill-favored.

A page — a young male servant — came from inside the house and said, "Come inside, gentle Mr. Slender, come inside; we are waiting for you."

"I'll eat nothing," Slender said. "I thank you, sir."

"By cock and pie, you shall not choose, sir!" the page said. "You must accept this invitation! Come inside, come inside."

"Please, lead the way," Slender said to Anne Page.

"Come on, sir," the page said.

"Miss Anne, you shall go in first," Slender said.

"Not I, sir," Anne Page said. "Please, go in first."

"I'll rather be unmannerly than troublesome," Slender said. "You do yourself wrong, indeed!"

He went inside. Unseen by him, Anne Page followed him with her apron spread wide in her hands. She was acting as if she were driving a goose before her. The page, amused, followed her.

— 1.2 —

Sir Hugh Evans and Simple, Slender's manservant, came out of the Pages' house. Sir Hugh had instructions to give to Simple.

"Go your ways, and ask of the French Doctor Caius' house which is the way," Sir Hugh said.

He meant for Simple to ask for directions to Doctor Caius' house, but his English was so poor that it seemed that he was asking the page to ask Doctor Caius' house for directions.

He continued, "In Doctor Caius' house there dwells one Mistress Quickly, which is in the manner of [who is] his nurse, or his dry nurse, or his cook, or his laundry [laundress], his washer, and his wringer."

Clothing was wrung to remove excess water after being washed.

Sir Hugh was unintentionally funny when he said that Mistress Quickly was Doctor Caius' "nurse." A nurse is a housekeeper, which is what Mistress Quickly was, but the juxtaposition with "dry nurse" called to mind a wet nurse and the image of Doctor Caius paying Mistress Quickly to breastfeed him.

"Yes, sir," Simple said.

"Nay, it is petter [better] yet [I have more to tell you]," Sir Hugh said. "Give her this letter; for it [she] is a 'oman that altogether's acquaintance [a woman who is thoroughly acquainted] with Miss Anne Page: and the letter is to desire and require [ask] her to solicit your master's desires to Miss Anne Page."

The purpose of the letter was to ask Mistress Quickly to say nice things about Slender to Anne Page in the hope that Anne Page would agree to marry him.

"Please, be gone," Sir Hugh said. "I will go back and make an end of my dinner; there's pippins and cheese to come. Apples and cheese make the perfect finish to a meal."

In a room at the Garter Inn, Falstaff, the Host of the Garter Inn, and Falstaff's followers Bardolph, Nym, and Pistol were talking. Also present was Falstaff's page, who was named Robin.

"My Host of the Garter!" Falstaff said.

"What says my bully-rook?" the Host replied. "What do you want, jolly fellow? Speak scholarly and wisely."

At the time, "bully" was not an insult. It meant "fine fellow" or "good friend."

"Truly, my Host, I must turn away and fire some of my followers," Falstaff said.

The Host thought that was a good idea: "Discard them, fire them, bully Hercules; cashier them. Let them depart; let them trot, trot away."

"The bill here for my followers and me is ten pounds a week."

"You are an Emperor — Caesar, Kaiser, and Vizier," the Host said. "I will hire Bardolph; he shall draw draughts of beer, and he shall tap barrels of beer and wine. Do I speak well, bully Hector?"

"Good idea," Falstaff said. "Hire Bardolph, my good Host."

"I have decided to do that," the Host said. "Let him follow me and obey my orders."

The Host said to Bardolph, "Let me see you froth and lime."

The Host wanted to begin training Bardolph to be a bartender immediately. To froth meant to pour beer in such a way that it had a large head; that way the customer would be paying for froth as well as beer. To lime meant to put lime in bad wine to mask the bad taste. Both frothing and liming were ways to cheat customers.

The Host said to Bardolph, "I have nothing more to say. Follow me."

The Host left the room.

"Bardolph, follow him," Falstaff said. "A tapster — being a bartender — is a good trade. An old cloak will provide material for a new jacket; a withered manservant can become a fresh and new tapster. Go; *adieu*."

"It is a life that I have desired," the alcoholic Bardolph said. "This is my dream job. I will thrive."

Pistol declaimed, "Oh, base Hungarian wight! Will you the spigot wield? Oh, base and hungry beggar fellow! Will the spigot now be your weapon?"

Nym joked, "Bardolph was begotten by drunken parents, and so this is his dream job. Isn't that a humorous conceit?"

"I am glad I am so rid of this tinderbox," Falstaff said. "A tinderbox contains materials to start a fire, and Bardolph's red nose is burning. His thefts were too open; his filching was like an unskillful singer — he kept not time. There is a right time to steal — a time when you won't likely be caught. There is also a wrong time to steal — a time when you will likely be caught."

Nym said, "The good humor is to steal at a minute's rest — the best time to steal is to commit a theft in the shortest possible time."

Pistol said, "The wise don't call it stealing; they use the euphemism of 'conveying,' as in conveying money from someone else's pocket to your pocket. 'Steal'! This is what I think of that word!"

He made a rude gesture with his middle finger.

"Well, sirs," Falstaff said, "I am almost out at heels."

He meant that he was almost broke, but Pistol took the expression "out at heels" literally — he pretended that Falstaff had holes in the heels of his stockings and that his shoes were almost worn out.

"Why, then, let blisters ensue," Pistol said.

"There is no remedy; I must cony-catch; I must shift," Falstaff said. "I must use my wits to come up with a way to get money."

"Young ravens must have food," Pistol said. Falstaff had been paying for the rooms and meals of his followers.

"Which of you know of Mr. Ford here in this town?" Falstaff asked.

Pistol replied, "I have heard of the fellow. He is rich."

"My honest lads," Falstaff said, "I will tell you what I am about."

Pistol pretended that Falstaff meant "round about" — his circumference.

He said, "Two yards, and more."

"No quips now, Pistol!" Falstaff said. "Indeed, I am in the waist two yards round about, but I am now about no waste; I am about thrift. Briefly, I intend to pursue Ford's wife. I spy entertainment in her; she discourses, she is always as affable as if she is carving meat for guests, she gives the leer of invitation. I can interpret the action of her familiar style, and I can translate it so that it can be easily understood. When I make the least favorable interpretation of her behavior and translate it into plain English, her behavior clearly says, 'I am Sir John Falstaff's.'"

By "least favorable," Falstaff meant "least favorable" to him. That is, he thought that if you looked at Mrs. Ford's behavior and noted what was least favorable to Falstaff, you would still have to conclude that Mrs. Ford was sexually attracted to him.

But "least favorable" could be interpreted as least favorable to Mrs. Ford. That is, if you looked at Mrs. Ford's behavior and interpreted it in the way that made Mrs. Ford look worst, you would conclude that Mrs. Ford was sexually attracted to Falstaff.

Pistol said, "He has studied her will, and he has translated her will out of honesty into English."

Pistol's words stated that Falstaff had studied Mrs. Ford's will — that is, her desires — and he was honestly translating, or interpreting, her hidden desires into plain English — that is, something that could easily be understood.

According to Falstaff, Mrs. Ford was sexually attracted to him. Falstaff thought that his interpretation of Mrs. Ford's desires was correct.

Pistol's words, however, had a secondary meaning. Pistol was also saying that Falstaff had studied Mrs. Ford's will — that is, her desires — and he was translating, or interpreting, her desires, which were honest, aka chaste, aka faithful to her husband, as being ingle-ish toward Falstaff. Now obsolete, the phrase "to ingle" meant "to fondle or caress." An ingle was a paramour — a lover who was married to someone else.

According to Pistol, Mrs. Ford was faithful to her husband, and Falstaff was wrong when he thought that Mrs. Ford was sexually attracted to him. Pistol thought that Falstaff's interpretation of Mrs. Ford's desires was incorrect. So did Nym.

"The anchor is deep," Nym said. "Will that humor pass? Does that expression make sense?"

Does the expression "the anchor is deep" make sense in this context? You decide.

An anchor that has been dropped into the sea keeps the ship from moving very far. Perhaps Nym meant that Falstaff's plans for Mrs. Ford would not go very far.

Falstaff said, "I have heard gossip that Mrs. Ford controls her husband's purse. Mr. Ford has a legion of angels; he has many angels — coins imprinted with a depiction of the archangel Michael."

"As many Devils entertain; and 'To her, boy,' say I," Pistol said.

He meant that Falstaff should seek the assistance of as many Devils as Mrs. Ford had angels.

"The humor rises — this conversation grows more interesting," Nym said. "It is good. Humor me the angels — find a way to get the money and give me some of it."

Even if Falstaff's plot were poor, Nym would not mind benefitting from it if — against the odds — it should work.

"I have here a letter that I have written to her," Falstaff said, "and here I have another letter that I have written to Mr. Page's wife, who just now also eyed me thoroughly. She examined my parts with most judicious ogles and amorous glances; sometimes she shot beams of eyesight at my foot, and sometimes at my portly belly."

"Then did the Sun on a dunghill shine," Pistol said.

"I thank you for that humor," Nym said to Pistol. "That was an appropriate expression for this occasion."

Neither Nym nor Pistol objected to getting money from the Fords; neither Nym nor Pistol thought that Falstaff had much of a chance of seducing either Mrs. Ford or Mrs. Page.

"Oh, Mrs. Page did so run her amorous glances over my exterior parts with such a greedy and intent observation that the appetite of her eye did seem to scorch me and burn me up like light falling on me after leaving a magnifying glass!" Falstaff said. "Here's another letter. This one is for Mrs. Page. She also controls her husband's money; she is a rich region in rich Guiana — she is all gold and bounty.

"I will be escheator to them both; I will be their treasury officer, and I will cheat them both. They shall be exchequers to me; they will be my treasuries. They shall be my East and West Indies, and I will trade with them and profit from them both.

"Go. One of you take this letter to Mrs. Page; and one of you take this letter to Mrs. Ford. We will thrive, lads; we will thrive."

Both Nym and Pistol objected to Falstaff's scheme. They thought that he had little or no chance of succeeding in seducing either Mrs. Ford or Mrs. Page.

Pistol said, "Shall I Sir Pandarus of Troy become, and by my side wear steel? Then, Lucifer take all! If I become a pander like that fellow who was the go-between of Troilus and Cressida, then I will lose honor as a soldier. No, I won't do it! I would rather go to Hell!"

"I will run no base humor," Nym said. "Here, take back the humor-letter: I will keep the 'havior of good reputation. I will act in such a way that I will not get a bad reputation as a pander."

Falstaff said to Robin, his page, "Deliver these letters quickly, and sail like my pinnace — my small ship — to these golden shores. You can be the small ship that accompanies me, the big ship."

He then said to Nym and Pistol, "Rogues, get you hence, avaunt! Vanish like hailstones, go. Trudge, plod away on the hoof; seek shelter, pack off! You are fired!

"I, Falstaff, will learn the humor of the age," Falstaff said, "and the custom of the age is French thrift, you rogues. From now on, my household will consist of myself and my uniformed page."

Pistol and Nym now had to fend for themselves — Falstaff would no longer pay for their room and board.

Falstaff left the room.

Pistol shouted after Falstaff, "Let vultures gripe your guts! Gourd and fullam — two kinds of loaded dice — rule, and high and low numbers beguile rich and poor men.

"I'll have money in my wallet when you are broke, you base Phrygian Turk!"

Nym said to Pistol, "I have operations that are humors of revenge. I want to get revenge on Falstaff."

"Will you really get revenge?" Pistol asked.

"Yes, by welkin — the sky — and her star!" Nym said.

The star is the Sun.

"Will you get revenge with wit — intelligence — or with steel swords?" Pistol asked.

"With both the humors, I will," Nym said. "I will discuss the humor of this love with Mr. Page. I will tell him what Falstaff plans to do with his wife."

"And I to Mr. Ford shall eke — also — unfold," Pistol said, "how Falstaff, that varlet vile, his dove will prove, his gold will hold, and his soft couch defile. I will tell Mr. Ford what Falstaff plans to do with his wife."

"I will do more," Nym said. "My humor shall not cool. I will incense Page to deal with poison. I will possess him with the color of jealousy. I will make him want to attack Falstaff. This revolt of mine is dangerous — that is my true humor and that is truly the way I feel about it."

"You are the Mars of malcontents," Pistol said. "You are the most warlike of malcontents, and you make a dangerous enemy. I will follow you. Lead on."

They left to find Mr. Ford and Mr. Page.

In a room of the house of the French Doctor Caius, Mistress Quickly was talking with Slender's manservant Peter Simple. Also present was Doctor Caius' manservant John Rugby.

Mistress Quickly did not want Doctor Caius to know that Simple was in his house. She said, "John Rugby, please go to the window, and see if you can see our master, Doctor Caius, coming. If he comes in and finds anybody in the house, truly there will be plenty of abusing of God's patience and the King's English."

"I'll go and watch for him," Rugby said.

"Go; and we'll have a posset — hot milk curdled with ale or wine — as a reward for the troubles we take now. We will drink a posset very soon tonight, truly, at the latter end — the embers — of a sea-coal fire."

Doctor Caius was wealthy. He could afford to burn high-quality coal shipped in by sea.

Rugby went to the window.

Mistress Quickly said, "Rugby is an honest, willing, kind fellow, as ever any servant who shall be in a house, and, I promise you, he is no tell-tale, aka tattle-tale, nor no breed-bate, aka trouble-maker. Rugby's worst fault is that he is given to prayer; he is something peevish — perverse and headstrong — that way. But everyone has a fault, so let us allow this fault to pass."

She added, "Peter Simple, did you say your name is?"

"Yes, for fault of a better," Simple said.

"And Mr. Slender is your master?"

"Yes, indeed."

"Doesn't he wear a great round beard, like a glover's paring-knife?"

A glover's paring-knife was flat and round and was used for smoothing leather. Glovers worked with leather to make gloves and other items.

"No, he does not," Simple said. "He has only a little wee face, with a little yellow beard, a Cain-colored beard. His beard is the color of the beard of Cain, the first murderer, as recounted in the Bible."

"He is a softly spirited — gentle — man, isn't he?" Mistress Quickly asked.

"Yes, he is," Simple said, "but he is as tall a man of his hands as any is between this and his head — he is as valiant a man as any in this region. He has fought with a warrener."

A warrener was a gamekeeper who kept rabbits. Apparently, Slender had gotten into a fight after being caught poaching rabbits.

"Do you say! Oh, I should remember him! Doesn't he hold up his head, like this, and strut in his gait?"

Mistress Quickly imitated him well enough that Simple knew that she was imitating Slender.

"Yes, indeed, he does those things," Simple said.

"Well, may Heaven send Anne Page no worse fortune! Tell Master Parson Evans I will do what I can for your master: Slender. I will help him court her. Anne is a good girl, and I wish —"

Rugby said, "Here comes Doctor Caius!"

"We shall be caught and scolded!" Mistress Quickly said.

She pointed to Doctor Caius' study and said to Simple, "Run in here, good young man. Go into this study; he — Doctor Caius — will not stay long."

Simple went into the study and Mistress Quickly shut the door.

Mistress Quickly said loudly so that Doctor Caius would hear her, "John Rugby! Go, John, go and look for our master; I think that he must not be well because he has not come home."

She began to sing, "And down, down, adown-a ...."

The heavily accented French Doctor Caius entered his house and said, "Vat [What] is you sing? I do not like des [these] toys [things that are foolish nonsense]. Please, go and vetch [fetch] me in [from] my study *un boitier vert* [a green box], a box, a green-a box. Do intend [you understand] vat I speak? A green-a box."

"Yes, I'll fetch it for you," Mistress Quickly said.

She thought, *I am glad he did not look in the study himself; if he had found the young man, he would have been horn-mad.*

A person who is horn-mad is a person who is as mad as a horned animal during mating season — or as mad as a husband who has just discovered that he has been cuckolded.

"*Ja foi, il fait fort chaud. Je m'en vais a la cour — la grande affaire!*" Doctor Caius said.

This meant, "In faith, it is very hot. I am going to the court — a grand affair!"

"Is this the box you want, sir?" Mistress Quickly asked.

"*Oui; mette le au mon pocket.* [Yes; put it in my pocket.] *Depeche* [Be quick], quickly. Vere [Where] is dat [that] knave Rugby?"

Mistress Quickly called, "John Rugby! John!"

Rugby said, "Here I am, sir!"

Doctor Caius said, "You are John Rugby, and you are Jack Rugby. Come, take-a your rapier, and come after my heel to the court."

A Jack is a knave or rascal; Jack, of course, is also a nickname for a person named John.

Rugby said, "The rapier is ready, sir; it is here on the porch."

"By my trot [troth, aka faith or truth], I tarry too long," Doctor Caius said. "'od's me! [God's me! = God saves me!] *Qu'ai-j'oublie*? [What have I forgotten?] Dere [There] is some simples in my study, dat [that] I vill [will] not for the varld [world] I shall leave behind."

One meaning of "trot" is "old woman." Simples are medicines made from one plant or herb.

Doctor Caius went into his study.

Mistress Quickly, "Ah, me, he'll find the young man there, and he'll be mad!"

"Oh, *diable, diable!* [Oh, Devil, Devil!] Vat [What] is in my study? Villain! *Larron!* [Thief!]"

He pulled Simple out of his study and called, "Rugby, bring me my rapier!"

"Good master, be calm and peaceful," Mistress Quickly said.

"Wherefore shall I be calm-a and peaceful-a?"

"The young man is an honest man," Mistress Quickly said.

"What shall de [the] honest man do in my study? Dere [There] is no honest man dat [that] shall come in my study."

"Please, don't be so phlegmatic. Hear the truth: He came to me on an errand from Parson Hugh."

Mistress Quickly was misusing a word. Instead of the word "phlegmatic," which means "unemotional and calm," she should have used the word "choleric," which means "angry."

"Vell [Well]," Doctor Caius said.

"Yes, truly," Simple said. "My master wants Mistress Quickly to —"

"Be quiet, please," Mistress Quickly said. Doctor Caius wanted to marry Anne Page, and he would be even angrier if he learned about a rival for her.

"Peace-a your tongue," Doctor Caius said to Mistress Quickly.

He said to Simple, "Speak-a your tale."

"My master wants this honest gentlewoman, your maid, Mistress Quickly, to speak a good word to Miss Anne Page about my master in the way of marriage."

"This is all he wants, indeed," Mistress Quickly said. She added, "But I'll never put my finger in the fire, without need."

She was saying to Doctor Caius that she would not say good things about Slender to Anne Page, although she had told Simple that she would.

"Sir Hugh send-a you?" Doctor Caius said to Simple.

He added, "Rugby, *baille* [bring] me some paper."

He said to Simple, "Tarry you a little-a while."

Doctor Caius began to write a note.

Mistress Quickly whispered to Simple, "I am glad he is so quiet. If he had been thoroughly moved, you should have heard him yelling so loud and so melancholy [Mistress Quickly meant 'choleric,' aka angry, rather than 'melancholy,' which she used instead of 'melancholic']. But notwithstanding, man, I'll do you and your master what good I can: and the very yea and the no is, the French doctor, my master — I may call him my master, you see, for I keep his house; and I wash, wring, brew, bake, scour, dress meat [prepare food] and drink, make the beds and do everything by myself —"

Simple whispered to Mistress Quickly, "It is a great charge — burden or responsibility — to come under one body's hand."

Mistress Quickly whispered to Simple, "Do you know that? I can tell you that it is true. I am up early and down late; but notwithstanding — to tell you in your ear, I would have no words spoken aloud about it — my master himself is in love with Miss Anne Page, but notwithstanding that, I know Anne's mind — that's neither here nor there."

Doctor Caius said to Simple, "You jack'nape [jackanapes, aka ape], give-a this letter to Sir Hugh; by gar [God], it is a shallenge [challenge]. I will cut his troat [throat] in dee [the] park; and I will teach a scurvy jack-a-nape priest to meddle or make. You may be gone; it is not good that you tarry here. By gar, I will cut [off] all his two stones [testicles]; by gar, he shall not have a stone to throw at his dog."

Carrying Doctor Caius' note, Simple left.

Mistress Quickly said to Doctor Caius, "Sir Hugh was simply trying to help his friend Slender."

"It is no matter-a ver dat [for that]," Doctor Caius said. "Do not you tell-a me dat [that] I shall have Anne Page for myself? By gar, I vill [will] kill de [the] Jack [rascal] priest; and I have appointed mine [the] Host of de Jarteer [Garter Inn] to measure our weapons. By gar, I will myself have Anne Page."

Doctor Caius wanted the Host of the Garter Inn to officiate at the duel of Sir Hugh and Doctor Caius. Among other things, the Host of the Garter Inn would measure their swords to make sure that they are equal in length. If one person's sword was longer than the other person's, the person with the longer sword would have an advantage in the duel.

"Sir, the maiden — Anne Page — loves you," Mistress Quickly said, "and all shall be well. We must give folks leave to prate and gossip. Heavens!"

Doctor Caius said, "Rugby, come to the court with me."

He said to Mistress Quickly, "By gar, if I have not Anne Page, I shall turn your head out of my door. "

He added, "Follow my heels, Rugby."

He and Rugby walked out the door.

Mistress Quickly shouted after him, "You shall have Anne —" and then in a lower voice she said, "— an ass' head of your own. No, I know Anne's mind for all that. Never a woman in Windsor knows more of Anne's mind than I do; nor can do more than I do with her, I thank Heaven."

Fenton arrived and called, "Is anyone at home?"

"Who's there, I wonder?" Mistress Quickly said. "Come inside the house, please."

Fenton entered the room and asked, "How are you now, good woman? How are you doing?"

"I am doing better than before because it pleases your good worship to ask," Mistress Quickly replied. "I am glad that you are courteous enough to ask me how I am doing."

"What is the news?" Fenton asked. "How is pretty Miss Anne doing?"

"Truly, sir, she is pretty, and honest, and gentle; and one who is your friend, I can tell you that by the way," Mistress Quickly said. "I praise Heaven for it."

"Shall I do any good if I woo her, do you think?" Fenton asked. "Won't she refuse my offer to marry her?"

"Truly, sir, all is in His hands above," Mistress Quickly replied. "But notwithstanding, Mr. Fenton, I'll be sworn on a book, she loves you. Don't you have a wart above your eye?"

Fenton was wearing a hat, and so Mistress Quickly could not see if he had a wart.

"Yes, I have, but what of that?"

"Well, thereby hangs a tale," Mistress Quickly said. "Truly, Anne is a remarkably charming girl. I detest [Mistress Quickly meant 'confess'] that she is as virtuous a maiden as ever broke bread. We talked for an hour about that wart. I shall never laugh but in that maiden's company! But indeed she is given too much to allicholy [Mistress Quickly meant 'melancholy'] and musing. But when it comes to you — well, never mind."

The word "melancholy" does not seem to accurately describe Anne.

"Well, I shall see her today," Fenton said. "Wait, here's some money for you; let me have your voice speaking in my behalf. If you see her before I see her, tell her good things about me."

"Will I do that?" Mistress Quickly said. "Truly, you and I both will; and I will tell you more about what we said about the wart the next time you and I have confidence [a private conversation]; and I will tell you about Anne's other wooers."

"Farewell," Fenton said. "I am in a great hurry now."

"Farewell to you," Mistress Quickly said.

Fenton departed, and Mistress Quickly said to herself, "Truly, he is an honest and virtuous gentleman, but Anne does not love him. I know that because I know Anne's mind as well as another person does."

So Mistress Quickly thought, but the person who knew whom Anne Page loved was Anne Page herself.

Mistress Quickly said, "Darn! I have forgotten something!"

She departed.

CHAPTER 2

— 2.1 —

On a street in Windsor, Mrs. Page stood looking at Falstaff's love letter to her.

She said to herself, "Have I escaped love letters in the holiday-time of my beauty — when I was young — and am I now a subject for them? Let me see."

She read Falstaff's letter to her out loud:

"*Ask me for no reason why I love you; for although Love may use Reason for his physician, he admits him not for his counselor. Yes, Love can consult Reason, yet Love need not accept Reason's advice. You are not young, and I am young no more. In this, we have something in common. You are merry, and so am I: Ha, ha! In this, we have something else in common. You love wine, and so do I. Can you wish to have anything else in common with a man?*

"*Let it suffice you, Mrs. Page — at the least, if the love of a soldier can suffice — that I love you. I will not say, 'Pity me'; it is not a soldier-like phrase to say: 'Pity me.' But I do say, 'Love me.' By me,*

"*Thine own true knight,*

"*By day or night,*

"*Or any kind of light,*

"*With all his might*

"*For you to fight.*

"*Signed, JOHN FALSTAFF.*"

"For you to fight" was ambiguous. It could mean that Falstaff was ready to fight for Mrs. Page, or it could mean that Mrs. Page would fight with Falstaff.

She looked up from the letter and said, "What a Herod of Jewry is this! The character Herod rants and raves on the stage, and Falstaff makes as much sense in this letter as Herod does in the theater. Oh, wicked world! Falstaff is well-nigh worn to pieces with age, and he is attempting to act like a young gallant!

"Falstaff resembles the Flemish — they are potbellied drunkards! And somehow this Flemish drunkard has looked at my behavior while I was around and picked out something that he considers unweighed — imprudent. When he picked out that unweighed something, he was picking out the Devil's name!

And now because of that unweighed something — whatever it was — he dares in this manner to proposition me! What should I say to him? Whenever I was around him, I was frugal with my mirth. I did nothing wrong, and Heaven forgive me for what I am now thinking! Why, I am tempted to push for a bill in the Parliament for the putting down of men! How shall I be revenged on this Falstaff? I will be revenged on him as surely as his guts are stuffed with sausages."

Mrs. Ford arrived, seeking Mrs. Page for advice.

"Mrs. Page!" she called. "Believe me, I was just going to your house."

"And, believe me, I was coming to visit you," Mrs. Page said. "You look very ill."

"No, I will never believe that I look ill in the sense of being ugly," Mrs. Ford said. The letter she had received from Falstaff had upset her, but she was still able to make jokes. "I have evidence to show the contrary." She meant that the love letter was evidence that she was not ugly.

"Truly, you do look ill, in my opinion," Mrs. Page said.

"Well, I do then," Mrs. Ford said, "yet I say I could show you evidence to the contrary. Oh, Mrs. Page, give me some advice!"

"What's the matter, woman?"

"If it were not for one trifling thing, I could come to quite a lot of 'honor'!"

"If it is only a trifling thing, forget about it, and take the honor," Mrs. Page replied. "What is the matter? Dispense with trifles. What is the matter?"

"If I would only be willing to go to Hell for an eternal moment or so, I could be knighted," Mrs. Ford said.

She meant — and believed — that if she committed adultery with Falstaff, she would go to Hell eternally. Each moment would last an eternity. As for being knighted by Falstaff, she would be benighted — she would be doing night-work during the night with a knight on top of her. This was not an 'honor' she desired.

"What? You must be joking!" Mrs. Page said. "You say that you would be Sir Alice Ford!"

She was able to guess what had happened: Mrs. Page had received a letter similar to the letter that she had received and written by the same knight who had written her letter.

Mrs. Page said, "These knights will hack; and so you should not alter the article of your gentry."

Knights can hack with their swords, and they can also use their "swords" to do other things — say, to a woman in bed. At the time, "hackney" was slang for a prostitute as well as a word that referred to horses. Horses and prostitutes are both ridden. Mrs. Page was telling Mrs. Ford that knights can be promiscuous and therefore she ought not to seek any change in her gentry — her social status.

"We burn daylight," Mrs. Ford said. "We are wasting time. Here, take this letter and read it; you will perceive how I might be knighted. I shall think the worse of fat men, as long as I have an eye to see distinctions such as fat and thin in the bodies of men.

"Yet Falstaff did not swear and curse. He praised women's modesty, and he gave such orderly and well-behaved reproof to all manner of uncomeliness, to all unethical actions, that I would have sworn his disposition would have gone to the truth of his words. He talks like a gentleman, but when you read this letter, you will see that he does not write like one.

"The way he talks and the way he writes go together no more or better than Psalm One Hundred — a hymn of praise of God — goes together with the secular heartbreak song 'Greensleeves'!"

These are two lyrics of 'Greensleeves': "Alas, my love, you do me wrong / To cast me off discourteously!" Psalm One Hundred states, in part, "For the Lord is good; His mercy is everlasting."

Mrs. Ford continued, "What tempest, what storm, I wonder, threw this whale, with so many barrels of oil in his big belly, ashore at Windsor? How shall I get revenge on him? I think the best way would be to fill him with hope that he could sleep with me. I could tease him until the wicked fire of his lust has melted him in his own grease. Did you ever see the like of that letter?"

"Indeed, I have," Mrs. Page said. "Letter for letter the same, except that the name of Page and Ford differs! I can provide you great comfort in this mystery of how Falstaff conceived an ill opinion of you — and me. Here's the twin brother of your letter. It is exactly the same as your letter except that it has my name in it.

"I am willing to let your letter receive the inheritance the way that the eldest brother inherits the property in primogeniture. I swear that my letter will inherit nothing that belongs to Falstaff.

"I would be willing to bet that he has a thousand of these letters, all written with blank spaces left where he can write different names. In addition, I am willing to bet that the letters we received are from the second edition — he has already used up all the letters printed in the first edition. I don't doubt that he has printed so many 'love' letters that he needs a second edition. He does not care what he puts into the printing press or another kind of press — he wants to put us two in bed so that he can press us with his weight. I would prefer to be a giantess, and lie under Mount Pelion with the giants Otus and Ephialtes, who tried to reach Mount Olympus and make war against the gods. Their plan was to pile mountains on top of Mount Olympus; however, the Olympian gods defeated them and piled the mountains on top of Otus and Ephialtes. Our being under Falstaff's belly in bed would be worse than being buried under mountains.

"Well, I can find twenty promiscuous turtledoves before I can find one chaste man. Turtledoves are known for being faithful to their mates, so I will never find twenty promiscuous turtledoves."

Mrs. Ford, who had been comparing the two letters, said, "Why, your letter is the same as my letter; it has the very same handwriting and the very same words. What does he think about us that makes him send these letters to us?"

"I don't know, but it must be bad," Mrs. Page said. "It makes me almost ready to act contrary to my own honesty and chasteness. I am almost tempted to regard myself as someone with whom I am not acquainted. Surely, unless he knows about some evil strain in me that I myself do not know, he would never have tried to board me in this violent way. It is as if he were a pirate trying to violently board a ship."

"'Boarding,' you call it?" Mrs. Ford said. "I'll be sure to keep him above deck."

"So will I," Mrs. Page said. "If he ever comes under my hatches, I'll never go to sea again.

"Let's be revenged on him. Let's appoint a time for a meeting with him. We will pretend that we are interested in him and we will lead him on with bait, but we will delay and delay what he wants. We will lead him on until he has pawned his horses to the Host of the Garter Inn in order to pay for his sexual pursuit of us. We will hurt him in his wallet and perhaps in other places."

"I will be willing to act in any villainous way against Falstaff," Mrs. Ford said, "as long as it does not sully our carefully guarded honesty and chasteness. If my husband were to see this letter, it would give him eternal grounds for his jealousy."

"Look, your husband is coming here, and my husband, too," Mrs. Page said. "My good husband is as far from jealousy as I am from giving him cause to be jealous, and that I hope is an immeasurable distance."

"You are the happier woman because your husband is not jealous," Mrs. Ford said.

"Let's make plans together against this greasy knight," Mrs. Page said. "Come over here and let's talk."

They went to a shady place and talked, and Mr. Ford arrived, accompanied by Pistol, and Mr. Page arrived, accompanied by Nym. Pistol and Nym had been telling the two husbands about Falstaff's plans to seduce their wives.

Mr. Ford said to Pistol, "Well, I hope that it is not so."

"Hope is a curtal dog in some affairs," Pistol replied. "Sir John is after your wife."

A curtal dog is a dog with a docked — cut-off — tail. A curtal dog lacks something, and hope can be lacking in some affairs — sometimes, hope is not enough. Mr. Ford was hoping that his wife was faithful to him. She was, but Mr. Ford was jealous and Pistol's words were increasing Mr. Ford's jealousy.

"Why, sir, my wife is not young," Mr. Ford replied.

"Falstaff woos both highly born and lowly born, both rich and poor, both young and old, one with another, Mr. Ford," Pistol replied. "He loves the gallimaufry — he loves a stew made with every ingredient. Ford, perpend — pay attention."

"Falstaff loves my wife!"

"Yes," Pistol said, "with his passion burning hot. Prevent Falstaff's seduction of her, or you will find yourself like Actaeon with Ringwood, his dog, at his heels! Actaeon earned an odious name."

Actaeon was an ancient Greek hunter who saw the goddess Artemis bathing naked in a stream while he was hunting deer. Artemis is a militant virgin. Not pleased that Actaeon had seen her naked, she turned him into a horned stag and his own dogs chased him down and killed him. Because of the horns on Actaeon's head, he was later associated with cuckoldry and earned the name of cuckold. Cuckolds have unfaithful wives, and depictions of cuckolds show them with horns on their head.

"What name, sir?" Mr. Ford asked.

Pistol replied, "The name of the horn, I say. Farewell. Take heed and keep your eyes open because thieves do set foot by night. Take heed, before summer comes or cuckoo-birds sing."

Cuckoo-birds lay their eggs in other birds' nests, and so their young are taken care of by other birds' parents — a cuckold can end up raising another man's child. From the cry of the cuckoo came the word "cuckold."

Pistol said, "Let's go now, Sir Corporal Nym!"

He added, "Believe what Corporal Nym told you, Mr. Page; he speaks sense."

Mr. Ford thought, *I will patiently investigate this; I will find out whether this information is true.*

Nym said to Mr. Page, "And this is true; I like not the humor of lying. Falstaff has wronged me in some humors: I should have borne the humored letter to her; but I have a sword and it shall bite upon my necessity — it shall wound if I need to fight someone. Falstaff loves your wife; there's the short and the long of it. My name is Corporal Nym; I speak and I avouch that what I have said is true: My name is Nym, and Falstaff loves your wife. *Adieu.* I love not the humor of bread and cheese, and there's the humor of it. *Adieu.*"

Bread and cheese were meager rations — the absolute necessities. Nym was saying that he had gotten only bread and cheese while serving Falstaff, and now he meant to search for something better.

Pistol and Nym departed.

Mr. Page, who was amused by Nym's overuse of the word "humor," said to himself, "'The humor of it,' he said! Here's a fellow who frightens English out of its wits."

A short distance away from Mr. Page, Mr. Ford said to himself, "I will seek out Falstaff."

Mr. Page said to himself about Nym, "I never heard such a drawling, affected rogue. He drawls out his speeches by using repetitious and pretentious language."

Mr. Ford said to himself, "If I find that my wife is cheating on me, so be it."

Mr. Page said to himself, "I will not believe such a liar even if the priest of the town were to tell me that he is a true and honest man."

Mr. Ford said to himself, "He was a good sensible fellow."

Mr. Page said to his wife, "How are you, Meg?"

Mrs. Page and Mrs. Ford walked toward their husbands.

"Where are you going, George?" Mrs. Page asked her husband. "I need to know whether you will be home for the noon meal."

Mrs. Ford asked her husband, "How are you, sweet Frank! Why are you melancholy?"

"I melancholy!" Mr. Ford said. He lied, "I am not melancholy! Go home."

"Truly, you have some ideas in your head that make you melancholy," Mrs. Ford replied.

She asked, "Will you go with me, Mrs. Page?"

"Yes, I will," Mrs. Page replied.

Mrs. Page said to her husband, "Be sure to come to dinner, George."

She then whispered to Mrs. Ford, "Look who is coming yonder: Mistress Quickly. She shall be our messenger to this paltry knight: Falstaff."

Mrs. Ford whispered back, "Believe me, I was thinking about her. She will do the job."

Mrs. Page asked Mistress Quickly, "Have you come to see my daughter, Anne?"

"Yes, I have," Mistress Quickly replied. "How is she?"

"Come with us and see," Mrs. Page said. "We want to talk with you for an hour."

Mrs. Page, Mrs. Ford, and Mistress Quickly departed.

"How are you doing, Mr. Ford?" Mr. Page asked.

"You heard what this knave told me, didn't you?"

"Yes, and you heard what the other knave told me?"

"Do you think they were telling the truth?" Mr. Ford asked.

"Hang them both!" Mr. Page said. "They are low-lives. I do not think that Falstaff the knight would do this. These men who are accusing him of trying to seduce our wives are two of his discarded men; they are rogues now that they do not have jobs."

"Were they his men?" Mr. Ford asked.

"Yes, they were."

"I don't like what I heard any better for that. Is Falstaff staying at the Garter Inn?"

"Yes, he is," Mr. Page said. "If he really does intend this voyage of seduction towards my wife, I will turn her loose on him; and if he gets anything more from her than sharp words, let it lie on my head."

"I do not mistrust my wife," Mr. Ford said, "but I would be loath to allow her and Falstaff to be together. A man may be too confident. I would have nothing — and certainly not horns! — lie on my head: I cannot be as satisfied as you are."

The Host of the Garter Inn came walking toward them.

Mr. Page said, "Here comes the ranting Host of the Garter Inn. He has either liquor in his brain or money in his pocket when he looks so merry."

He said, "How are you, Host!"

"How are you, bully-rook!" the Host said. "You are a gentleman."

He called, "*Cavaleiro*-Justice, I say!"

The Host was bringing news of a duel, so he used the word *cavaleiro* to refer to Justice Shallow. *Cavaleiro* is a Spanish word referring to a knight on horseback or a courtly gentleman.

Justice Shallow, who had been walking behind the Host, walked up to the group of men and said, "I am coming, Host, I am coming."

He added, "Good day and twenty, good Mr. Page! Twenty-one good-days to you! Mr. Page, will you go with us? We have an entertainment at hand."

The Host said, "Tell him, *cavaleiro*-Justice; tell him, bully-rook."

Justice Shallow said to Mr. Page, "Sir, there is a fray to be fought between Sir Hugh the Welsh priest and Caius the French doctor."

Mr. Ford said, "Good Host of the Garter, may I speak to you?"

He and the Host went a short distance from the other men, and the Host asked, "What do you have to say to me, my bully-rook?"

Justice Shallow said to Mr. Page, "Will you go with us to watch the entertainment? My merry Host has had the measuring of their weapons; and, I think, he has sent them to different places so that they will not meet and fight each other. Believe me, I hear the parson is no jester. Listen, I will tell you what our entertainment shall be."

They talked together.

The Host asked, "Have you any suit against the knight Falstaff, my guest-*cavaleire*?"

"None, I say," Mr. Ford said, "but I'll give you a pottle — a half-gallon of mulled sack sweetened with burnt sugar if you give me access to him and tell him that my name is Brook; this is only for a jest."

Brook was a good name for Mr. Ford to choose; a brook is a small stream that is easily forded (crossed without a bridge).

"Let's shake hands," the Host said.

They shook hands.

The Host then said, "You shall have egress and regress; these are legal terms meaning the freedom to come and to go — did I use the right terms? And your name shall be Brook. Falstaff is a merry knight."

The Host then asked, "Will you go, gentlemen?"

Justice Shallow said, "I will go with you, Host."

Mr. Page said, "I have heard that the Frenchman has good skill with his rapier."

Justice Shallow said, "Tut, sir, I could have told you more about that. In these times fencers stand on distance, passes, stoccadoes, and I know not what. They pay attention to fancy stuff such as the space between fencers, lunges at each other, and thrusts at each other, but what is really important is in the heart, Mr. Page — that is what is important. In my day, back when I was young, I would have made all four of you stout-hearted fellows skip away like rats."

"Here, boys, here, here!" the Host said. "Shall we go?"

"I will go with you," Mr. Page said. "I would rather hear them scold each other than fight each other."

The Host, Justice Shallow, and Mr. Page departed.

Mr. Ford said to himself, "Although Page is so steadfastly and foolishly confident despite his wife's frailty, yet I cannot put off my suspicion so easily. Earlier, my wife was in Falstaff's company at Mr. Page's house; and what they did there, I don't know. Well, I will look further into this matter, and I have a disguise that I can use to talk to Falstaff and find out what is going on. If I find out that my wife is honest and faithful to me, I have not wasted my time. And if I find out that my wife is not honest and faithful to me, I have not wasted my time."

— 2.2 —

Falstaff and Pistol talked together in a room at the Garter Inn.

"I will not lend you a penny," Falstaff said.

"Why, then the world's my oyster, which I with sword will open," Pistol said. "I will have to make my living with my sword."

"Not a penny," Falstaff said. "I have allowed you, sir, to use your companionship with me to borrow money. I have begged my good friends for three reprieves for you and your coach-fellow Nym. If I had not, you two would have looking through prison bars, like two twin baboons. I am damned in Hell for swearing to gentlemen who are my friends that you two are good soldiers and brave fellows; and when Miss Bridget lost the valuable handle of her fan, I swore upon my honor that you did not have it."

"Didn't you get your fair share of the profit from the theft?" Pistol asked. "Didn't you get fifteen pence?"

"Use your reason, you rogue, use your reason," Falstaff replied. "Do you think that I would endanger my soul gratis — for free? Because I lied for you, my soul is in danger of spending eternity in Hell. In a word, hang no more around me — I am no gibbet for you. Go. A short knife and a throng of people is what you need! Be a cutpurse and a pickpocket! Cut the strings of a person's purse and put their money in your pocket! Go to your manor of Pickt-hatch, an unsavory part of London! Go.

"You told me that you will not bear a letter for me, you rogue! You told me that you insist upon your honor! Why, you unconfinable baseness — you boundless lowness — it is as much as I can do to keep the reputation of my own honor unstained.

"I myself sometimes, leaving the fear of God on the left hand so that it is out of my way and able to be ignored and hiding my honor in my necessity, am happy to shuffle, aka cheat; to hedge, aka deceive; and to lurch, aka dissemble; and yet you, you rogue, will hide your rags, your cat-a-mountain — wild — looks, your red-lattice, aka alehouse, speech and phrases, and your bold-beating oaths, under the shelter of your honor! You will not do it, you tell me!"

"I do relent," Pistol said. "I admit that you are right and I was wrong. What more do you want from a man?"

39

Falstaff's page, Robin, entered the room and said to Falstaff, "Sir, here is a woman who wants to speak with you."

"Let her in," Falstaff replied.

Mistress Quickly entered the room and said, "I wish you good morning."

Falstaff replied, "Good morning, good wife."

"That is not so, if it please your worship," Mistress Quickly said.

Falstaff knew that she was saying that she was not a wife, so he said, "Good maiden, then."

A maiden is an unmarried woman — a virgin.

"Yes, I swear that I am a maiden," Mistress Quickly said, "just as my mother was, the first hour I was born."

Mistress Quickly's speech frequently was mixed up. With the exception of Mother Mary, aka the Virgin Mary, a biological mother cannot be a virgin. Here, she was conflating two expressions: "a maiden as good as her mother" and "as innocent as a new-born babe."

"I do believe the swearer."

Falstaff was saying that he believed that Mistress Quickly was not a virgin.

He asked, "What do you want with me?"

"Shall I vouchsafe your worship a word or two?"

Again, Mistress Quickly's speech was mixed up. "To vouchsafe" means to grant, but she was not granting Falstaff a few words of conversation. She was requesting that he talk with her.

"You may speak two thousand words, fair woman," Falstaff said, "and I will vouchsafe you the hearing."

Falstaff knew the correct meaning of "vouchsafe."

"There is one Mrs. Ford, sir," Mistress Quickly said.

Worried that Pistol and Robin would overhear the conversation, she requested, "Please, come a little closer to me," and then she continued, "I myself dwell with master Doctor Caius —"

Still worried about Pistol and Robin overhearing the conversation, she hesitated, and Falstaff said, "Well, go on. Mrs. Ford, you say—"

"Yes," Mistress Quickly said. "Please, come a little closer to me."

"I promise you," Falstaff said, "that nobody hears us except people who are loyal to me."

"Are they?" Mistress Quickly asked. "May God bless them and make them His servants!"

"Well, what about Mrs. Ford?"

"Why, sir, she's a good creature. Lord! Lord! Your worship is a wanton — you are filled with lust! Well, may Heaven forgive you and all of us, I pray!"

"Come, what have you to tell me about Mrs. Ford?"

"Well, this is the short and the long of it," Mistress Quickly said. "You have brought her into such a canaries [Mistress Quickly meant 'quandary'] as is wonderful. The best courtier of them all, when the court was staying at Windsor, could never have brought her to such a canary [quandary]. Yet there has been knights, and lords, and gentlemen, with their coaches, I warrant you, coach after coach, letter after letter, gift after gift; smelling so sweetly, all perfumed with musk, and so rushling [Mistress Quickly meant 'rustling'], I promise you, in silk and gold; and in such alligant [Mistress Quickly meant 'eloquent and elegant'] terms; and in such wine and sugar of the best and the fairest, that would have won any woman's heart; and, I promise you, they could never get an eye-wink from her. I myself had twenty angels — coins — given to me as a bribe this morning; but I defy all angels, in any such sort, as they say, except those I get by way of honesty, and, I promise you, they could never get her to so much as sip on a cup of wine with the proudest of them all: and yet there has been Earls, nay, which is more, there has been pensioners; but, I promise you, all is one with her."

Mistress Quickly had said that pensioners were better than high-ranking Earls, something few, if any, people would agree with. Pensioners were old knights who received a pension, in return for which they attended chapel twice daily and prayed for the King.

Falstaff was an old knight to whom King Henry V had granted — or would grant — a pension.

Falstaff asked, "But what message is Mrs. Ford sending to me? Be brief, my good she-Mercury. Be brief, my good she-messenger."

Mercury is the main male messenger of the gods.

"She has received your letter, for the which she thanks you a thousand times; and she gives you to notify [she wants you to know] that her husband will be absence [absent] from his house between ten and eleven."

"Ten and eleven?"

"Yes, truly," Mistress Quickly said, and then you may come and see the picture, she says, that you know about."

One plausible reason for Falstaff to visit the Fords' home would be to see a noteworthy object such as a painting.

Mistress Quickly continued, "Mr. Ford, her husband, will be away from home then. Alas! The sweet woman leads an ill life with him. Mr. Ford is a very jealousy [jealous] man: She leads a very frampold, aka disagreeable, life with him, good heart."

"Between ten and eleven," Falstaff said. "Woman, commend me to her; I will not fail her — I will show up at that time."

"Why, you say well," Mistress Quickly said. "But I have another messenger to [message for] your worship. Mrs. Page has sent her hearty commendations to you, too, and let me tell you in your ear, she's as fartuous [Mistress Quickly meant 'virtuous'] a civil modest wife, and one, I tell you, who will not miss neither morning nor evening prayer, as any is in Windsor, whoever be the other civil modest wife here, and she bade me tell your worship that her husband is seldom away from home; but she hopes that there will come a time that he is absent. I never knew a woman so dote upon a man. I truly think you have magical charms, in truth."

These words by Mistress Quickly were ambiguous: "I never knew a woman so dote upon a man." Was Mrs. Page doting upon Falstaff — or her husband?

"Not I, I assure you," Falstaff said. "Setting the attractions of my good qualities — and looks — aside, I have no other charms."

"May God bless your heart for it!" Mistress Quickly said.

"But please tell me this," Falstaff said. "Has Ford's wife and Page's wife acquainted each other with how they love me?"

"That would be a jest indeed!" Mistress Quickly said. "They have not so little grace, I hope. That is a trick indeed! But Mrs. Page desires you to send to her your little page, of all loves. Her husband has a marvelous infection [Mistress Quickly meant 'affection'] for the little page; and truly Mr. Page is an honest man. Never a wife in Windsor leads a better life than she does: She does what she wants, says what she wants, buys what she wants with ready money, goes to bed when she wants, and rises when she wants — all is as she wants it to be, and truly she deserves it; because if there is a kind woman in Windsor, she is the one. You must send her your page; you must."

"Why, I will," Falstaff said.

"Be sure to do so," Mistress Quickly said. "Your page, look you, may come and go between you and Mrs. Page, and in any case have a password and other secret words so that you may know one another's mind, and the boy never needs to understand anything because it is not good that children should know any wickedness. Old folks, you know, have discretion, as they say, and know the world."

"Fare you well," Falstaff said. "Commend me to both Mrs. Ford and Mrs. Page. Here's some money for you, but it is not enough — I am still in your debt."

He said to Robin, his page, "Boy, go with this woman."

Mistress Quickly and Robin departed.

Falstaff said, "This news makes me distracted!"

Pistol said to himself about Mistress Quickly, "This punk, aka bawd or prostitute, is one of Cupid's carriers: She carries messages between people who want to be lovers. Clap on more sails, Pistol; pursue her; put your protective covering on, and fire at her. She will be my prize, or may the ocean overwhelm and drown us both!"

Pistol exited and went after Mistress Quickly.

Falstaff said to himself, referring to himself as Jack, "What do you think, old Jack? Continue on the path you are on. I'll make more of your old body than I have done. Will they — Mrs. Ford and Mrs. Page — yet look after you? Will you, after the expense of so much money, be now a gainer? I have spent so much money on food and drink to maintain you; now let Mrs. Ford and Mrs. Page provide money to maintain you — it is time that you brought me a profit. Good body, I thank you. Let anyone say that what I have done is grossly done; as long as it is in fact done, I don't care how it is done."

Bardolph, who was now working as a tapster at the Garter Inn, entered the room while carrying a cup of wine and said to Falstaff, "Sir John, there's a Master Brook below who would like to speak with you, and be acquainted with you; and he has sent your worship a morning's pick-me-up of wine."

"You said that Brook is his name?"

"Yes, sir."

"Bring him here."

Bardolph gave Falstaff the cup of wine and then departed.

Falstaff said to himself, "Such Brooks are welcome to me as long as they overflow with such liquor. Ha! Mrs. Ford and Mrs. Page, have I gotten you? Charge!"

Bardolph entered the room, leading Mr. Ford, who had disguised himself with a beard and who was carrying a bag of money. Falstaff had never seen Mr. Ford before, but Mr. Ford thought that later Falstaff might see him on a street and be introduced to him.

The disguised Mr. Ford said, "Bless you, sir!"

"And you, sir!" Falstaff replied, "Do you want to speak with me?"

"I make bold to press with so little preparation — advance warning — upon you."

"You're welcome here. What do you want?" Falstaff replied.

He said to Bardolph, "Leave us alone, drawer."

Bardolph exited.

Mr. Ford said, "Sir, I am a gentleman who has spent much money; my name is Brook."

"Good Mr. Brook, I hope to know you better."

"Good Sir John, I sue for your acquaintanceship. I do not want to put a load or any expense on you. I want you to know that I think myself more able to be a lender than you are. Knowing that to be true has somewhat emboldened me to this unseasonable intrusion; for they say, if money goes before, all ways do lie open."

"Money is a good soldier, sir, and it gets things done."

"That is true," Mr. Ford said, "and I have a bag of money here that burdens me. If you will help to bear it, Sir John, take half of it, or all of it. That will ease my burden of carrying it."

"Sir, I do not know what I have done to deserve to be your porter," Falstaff replied.

"I will tell you, sir, if you will give me the hearing."

"Speak, good Mr. Brook," Falstaff said. "I shall be glad to be your servant and listen to you."

"Sir, I hear you are a scholar — I will be brief with you — and you have been a man long known to me, although I had never as good an opportunity as I wanted to make myself acquainted with you. I shall reveal a thing to you, wherein I must very much lay open my own imperfection. But, good Sir John, as you have one eye upon my follies, as you hear them unfolded, turn your other eye upon the list of your own imperfections so that I may get by with a mild reproof, since you yourself know how easy it is to be such an offender."

"Very well, sir," Falstaff said. "Proceed."

"There is a gentlewoman in this town; her husband's name is Ford."

"Yes, that is true, sir."

"I have long loved her, and, I tell you sincerely, I have given her much; I have followed her with a doting observance; I have sought opportunities to meet her; I have taken advantage of every slight occasion that could even give me a glimpse of her; and I have not only bought many presents to give her, but also I have given much to many people in order to know what she would like to be given. In brief, I have pursued her as love has pursued me, which has been on the wing of all occasions.

"But whatever I have merited, either in my mind or through the use of my money and resources, I know that I have received no reward, unless experience is a jewel that I have purchased for an infinite amount, and that has taught me to say this: 'Love like a shadow flees when substance love pursues; pursuing that which flees, and flying what pursues.' In other words, 'Love, like a shadow, flees one pursuing and pursues one fleeing.'"

"Have you received any promise of satisfaction at her hands?" Falstaff asked.

"No. None. Never," Mr. Ford replied.

"Have you importuned her to such a purpose? Have you asked her for what you want?"

"Never."

"Of what quality is your love, then?"

"It is like a beautiful house that was built on another man's ground; I have lost my edifice by mistaking the place where I erected it," Mr. Ford said. "A house built on another man's ground belongs to the man who owns the land, not to the man who built the house."

"Why are you telling me all this?" Falstaff asked.

"When I have told you that, I have told you all. Some say that although Mrs. Ford appears to me to be honest and faithful to her husband, yet in other places she displays her mirth so much and so openly that malicious gossip is said about her. Now, Sir John, here is the heart of my purpose: You are a gentleman of excellent breeding, admirable discourse, of admittance into the company of the great, entitled to respect in your place and person, and universally approved of for your many war-like, court-like, and learned accomplishments."

"Oh, sir!" Falstaff said.

"Believe it, for you know it to be true," Mr. Ford said.

He gestured to the bag of money and said, "There is money; spend it, spend it; spend more; spend all I have. I ask only that you give me some of your time in exchange for the money. Give me as much time as it takes to lay an amiable siege to the honesty, aka virtue, of Mr. Ford's wife. Use your art of wooing and persuade her to consent to sleep with you. If any man can do that, you can as quickly as any other man."

"Would it apply well to the vehemence of your affection, that I should win what you would enjoy? I think that you prescribe to yourself very preposterously," Falstaff said. "Does it make sense for you to pay me to sleep with the woman whom you want to sleep with? Isn't that preposterous?"

"Oh, understand my meaning," Mr. Ford said. "She dwells so securely on the excellency of her honor, that the folly of my soul dares not present itself: She is too bright to be looked at. She claims to be so virtuous that I cannot approach her with my proposition.

"Now, if I could come to her with any evidence of her lack of virtue in my hand, my desires would have evidence and arguments to commend themselves. I could drive her then from the ward of her purity, her reputation, her marriage-vow, and her thousand other defenses, which now are very strongly embattled against me. She could no longer use her claims of virtue against me.

"What do you say to my proposition, Sir John?"

"Mr. Brook," Falstaff replied, "first, I will make bold with your money; next, give me your hand; and last, as I am a gentleman, you shall, if you wish, enjoy Ford's wife in bed."

"Oh, good sir!"

"I say you shall."

"You will not lack for money, Sir John; you will not lack for money."

"You will get Mrs. Ford, Mr. Brook," Falstaff said. "You will get her. You will not lack her.

"I shall be with her soon, I may tell you, by her own arrangement. Just before you came in to me, her assistant or go-between parted from me. I say that I shall be with Mrs. Ford between ten and eleven in the morning, for at that time the jealous rascally knave who is her husband will be away from home. Come to me later that night and you shall know how I succeed."

"I am blessed to know you," the disguised Mr. Ford said.

He added, "Do you know Mr. Ford, sir?"

"Hang him, that poor cuckoldly knave! I do not know him, yet I wrong him to call him poor; they say the jealous cuckoldly knave has masses of money; because of Mr. Ford's money, his wife seems to me especially good-looking. I will use her as the key of the cuckoldly rogue's coffer; and there's my harvest-home. Through his wife, I will get access to his money, and that will be the harvest of my seeding."

"I wish that you knew Mr. Ford, sir, so that you could avoid him if you saw him," the disguised Mr. Ford said.

"Hang him, the mechanical salt-butter rogue!" Falstaff said.

He had insulted Mr. Ford twice in that sentence. One, he called Mr. Ford a mechanical — a workingman. In their culture, a person who did not need to work to support himself had a higher social status than a person who had to work. Two, a person who ate inexpensive salted butter imported from Flanders had a lower social status than someone who could afford to eat English butter.

Falstaff continued, "I will flare at him and scare him out of his wits. I will awe him with my cudgel: it shall hang like a meteor over the cuckold's horns. It shall be over him, ready to fall, and it will be a sign of misfortune to come. Mr. Brook, you should know that I will predominate over the peasant, and you will sleep with his wife. Come to me at night after I have visited her in the morning. Mr. Ford is a knave, and I will add other disgraceful titles to that title. You, Mr. Brook, shall know that Mr. Ford is a knave and a cuckold. Come to me at night after I have visited her."

Falstaff took the money and departed.

Mr. Ford said to himself, "What a damned Epicurean —devoted to pleasure — rascal this Falstaff is! My heart is ready to crack with impatience. Who says my jealousy is unjustified? My wife sent a message to him; the hour for their meeting has been set; the match is made between them. Would any man have thought this? See the Hell of having a false — an unfaithful — woman! My bed shall be abused, my coffers ransacked, my reputation gnawn at; and I shall not only receive this villainous wrong, but I will also be called abominable names by the man who does me this wrong. Abominable names! Amaimon sounds well; Lucifer, well; Barbason, well — these are the names of Devils, the names of fiends of Hell. But what about the name of Cuckold! Or the name of Wittol — which is given to a contented cuckold! Cuckold! The Devil himself has not as bad a name as Cuckold! Page is an ass, an over-confident ass: He trusts his wife, and he is not jealous. I would rather trust a Flemish man with my butter, Parson Hugh the Welshman with my cheese, an Irishman with my bottle of whiskey, or a thief with walking my gentle gelding, than I would trust my wife with herself. If I were to trust her, then she would plot, then she would ruminate, then she would devise — and what wives think in their hearts they can do, they will break their hearts if they have to, but they will do it.

"May God be praised for my jealousy! Eleven o'clock is the hour that they will meet. I will prevent their adultery, get evidence of my wife planning to commit adultery, be revenged on Falstaff, and laugh at Page. I will start getting ready to do this; it is better to be three hours too soon than a minute too late.

"Damn! Damn! Damn! Cuckold! Cuckold! Cuckold!"

The following morning, the French Doctor Caius and his servant John Rugby stood in a field near Windsor. Duels were illegal, and so they were often fought in the morning. If they were fought later, they would attract more attention.

Doctor Caius called, "Jack Rugby!"

Rugby replied, "Sir?"

"Vat is de clock, Jack? [What is the time, Jack?]"

"It is past the hour, sir, that Sir Hugh promised to meet you and fight you in a duel."

"By gar [God], he has save his soul, dat [that] he is no come; he has pray his Pible [Bible] well, dat he is no come: by gar, Jack Rugby, he is [would be] dead already, if he be [had] come."

"He is wise, sir; he knew your worship would kill him, if he came."

"By gar, de herring is no dead so as I vill kill him. [By God, the herring is not as dead as I will kill him.] Take out your rapier, Jack; I vill [will] tell [Doctor Caius meant 'show'] you how I vill kill him."

"Alas, sir, I cannot fence."

"Villainy [Villain], take out your rapier."

"Stop! Here comes company."

The Host of the Garter Inn, Justice Shallow, Slender, and Mr. Page arrived.

The Host said to Doctor Caius, "Bless you, bully doctor!"

Justice Shallow said, "May God save you, Doctor Caius!"

Mr. Page said, "How are you now, good Doctor Caius!"

Slender said, "I wish you a good morning, sir."

"Vat be all you — one, two, tree [three], four — come for?"

The Host replied, "To see you fight, to see you foin, to see you traverse; to see you here, to see you there; to see you pass your punto, your stock, your reverse, your distance, your montant."

The Host was using a lot of fencing terms. To foin is to thrust. Traverse is a sideways thrust. Punto and stock are kinds of direct thrusts. Reverse is a backward thrust. Distance refers to keeping the proper amount of space between the two duelists. A montant is an upward thrust.

The Host added, "Is he dead, my Ethiopian? Is he dead, my François? Ha, bully! What says my Aesculapius? My Galen? My heart of elder? Is he dead, bully stale? Is he dead?"

The Host was referring to the duel that Doctor Caius was supposed to be having with Sir Hugh. Of course, the Host knew that Sir Hugh was not dead — the Host had sent him to a different field so that Sir Hugh and Doctor Caius would not hurt each other. In addition, the Host was calling Doctor Caius an Ethiopian because of his dark skin. Aesculapius and Galen were famous doctors of antiquity. The reference to the heart of elder was an insult. A heart of oak is a valiant heart — the oak is a hard wood. Wood from an elder tree is much softer than wood from an oak. Basically, the Host was having fun at the expense of Doctor Caius. He was deliberately using — and misusing — words that the Frenchman would not understand.

The word "stale" refers to urine. Doctors examined a patient's urine when determining the patient's state of health.

Doctor Caius replied, "By gar, he is de [the] coward Jack priest of de vorld; he is not [does not dare to] show his face."

A Jack is a knave.

The Host said, "You are a Castalion-King-Urinal. You are Hector of Greece, my boy!"

Again, the Host was insulting Doctor Caius. He called him a Castalion, aka Castilian, aka a native of Spanish descent. The English were very proud of their then-recent victory over the Spanish Armada. The Host also called Doctor Caius the King of the Urinals, again a reference to the doctor's use of analysis of urine in his medical practice. Finally, Hector of Greece was a joke by the Host. Hector was a Trojan, not a Greek. The Host was speaking quickly and piling on words that the French doctor was unlikely to understand.

Doctor Caius said to his four visitors, "Please, bear vitness [witness] that me [I] have stay [stayed] six or seven — two, tree [three] — hours waiting for him, and he is no come."

Doctor Caius was referring to waiting for Sir Hugh so that they could fight their duel. At first, he said that he had been waiting for six or seven hours, but seeing the looks of incredulity on his visitors' faces, he amended that to two or three hours.

Justice Shallow said, "He is the wiser man, Doctor Caius. He is a curer of souls, and you are a curer of bodies; if you should fight, you go against the hair of your professions."

To go against the hair meant to go against the grain. The expression referred to currying a horse: You should brush the horse's hair in the direction that the hair is growing.

Justice Shallow asked, "Isn't that true, Mr. Page?"

"Justice Shallow," Mr. Page replied, "you have yourself been a great fighter, although now you are a man of peace."

Justice Shallow replied, "Bodykins [By God's body], Mr. Page, though I now am old and of the peace, if I see a sword out, my finger itches to take part in the fight. Though we are justices and doctors and churchmen, Mr. Page, we have some salt — liveliness — of our youth in us; we are the sons of women, Mr. Page."

"That is true, Justice Shallow," Mr. Page said.

"It will be found so, Mr. Page," Justice Shallow said. "Doctor Caius, I am come to fetch you home. I am sworn to uphold the peace. You have showed yourself to be a wise physician, and Sir Hugh has shown himself a wise and patient churchman. You must go with me, Doctor Caius."

The Host said, "Pardon us, guest-Justice."

Justice Shallow, who was from Gloustershire, was visiting Windsor; he was staying at the Garter Inn.

The Host said to Doctor Caius, "A word, Monsieur Mock-water." They went a little distance away so that Justice Shallow could not hear them.

The Host had created the word "Mock-water" in mockery of Doctor Caius, who analyzed urine, which is sometimes called water.

"Mock-vater! Vat is dat?" Doctor Caius asked.

The Host replied, "Mock-water, in our English tongue, means valor or courage, bully."

"By gar, den, I have as mush [much] mock-vater as de [the, aka any] Englishman. Scurvy jack-dog priest! By gar, me vill [I will] cut [off] his ears."

"He will clapper-claw you tightly, bully."

"Clapper-de-claw! Vat is dat?"

The real meaning of "clapper-claw" was "beat" or "thrash" or "scratch" or "claw."

The Host said, "That is, he will make you amends."

"By gar, me do look he shall clapper-de-claw me; for, by gar, me vill have it."

"And I will provoke him to clapper-claw you," the Host said, "or let him wag — let him go to the Devil."

"Me tank [I thank] you for dat."

"And, moreover, bully — but first, Mr. guest-Justice, and Mr. Page, and eke [also] Cavaleiro Slender, go you through the town — Windsor — to Frogmore."

Frogmore was a small village on the other side of Windsor.

Mr. Page whispered to the Host, "Sir Hugh is there, isn't he?"

The Host whispered back, "He is there: see what humor — mood — he is in; and I will bring the doctor to him by way of the fields. You will arrive first. Is this OK?"

Justice Shallow whispered, "We will do it."

Mr. Page, Justice Shallow, and Slender all said out loud, "*Adieu*, good Doctor Caius."

They exited.

Doctor Caius said, "By gar, me vill [I will] kill de priest; for he speak for a jack-an-ape to Anne Page."

Doctor Caius was angry at Sir Hugh the priest because Sir Hugh was trying to convince Anne Page to marry Slender, whom Doctor Caius considered to be the equivalent of an ape.

"Let him die," the Host said. "Sheathe your impatience, throw cold water on your anger. Go through the fields with me beyond Frogmore. I will take you to where Miss Anne Page is; she is feasting at a farmhouse — and you shall woo her. The game you are hunting will then be in sight. Isn't that right?"

"By gar, me dank [I thank] you for dat," Doctor Caius said. "By gar, I respect you, and I shall procure-a you de good guest [guests]: de Earl, de knight, de lords, de gentlemen, my patients."

"For the which I will be your adversary toward Anne Page. Isn't that a good thing to say?"

Of course, the Host expected Doctor Caius to think that the Host would be his *advocate* — not adversary — with Anne Page.

"By gar, it is good; vell [well] said."

"Let us go, then," the Host said.

"Follow at my heels, Jack Rugby," Doctor Caius said.
They departed.

.

CHAPTER 3

— 3.1 —

The Welsh priest Sir Hugh Evans and Simple, who was Slender's servant, were in a field near Frogmore. They had been waiting for Doctor Caius to show up to fight a duel. Sir Hugh had a Bible in one hand and a sword in the other. Simple was holding Sir Hugh's cloak — a loose flowing upper garment.

Sir Hugh said, "I ask you now, good Mr. Slender's serving-man, and friend Simple by your name, which way have you looked for Master Caius, who calls himself doctor of physic [medicine]?"

"Sir, I have looked in the direction of Windsor Little Park, in the direction of Windsor Great Park, and in almost every direction, including in the direction of the village named Old Windsor. In fact, I have looked in every direction except in the direction of Windsor itself," Simple replied.

"I most fehemently [vehemently] desire you to also look that way."

"I will, sir."

Simple exited.

Sir Hugh's feelings were mixed up. He did not know whether to feel sad because he was about to fight a duel although he was a priest or to feel angry because he had reason to feel anger toward Doctor Caius.

He said to himself, "Pless [Bless] my soul, how full of chollors [cholers, aka angry feelings] I am, and trempling [trembling] of mind! I shall be glad if he have deceived me. How melancholies I am! I will knog his urinals about his knave's costard when I have good opportunities for the 'ork [work]. Pless my soul!"

By "I will knog his urinals about his knave's costard," Sir Hugh meant that he would knock the doctor's urinals — glass bottles in which urine was collected in order to be inspected — about his head.

Sir Hugh sang this:

"*To shallow rivers, to whose falls*

"*Melodious birds sings madrigals;*

"*There will we make our peds [beds] of roses,*

"*And a thousand fragrant posies.*

"*To shallow —*"

Then he stopped singing and said, "Mercy on me! I have a great dispositions to cry."

Then he sang this:

"*Melodious birds sing madrigals —*

"*When as I sat in Pabylon [Babylon] —*

"*And a thousand vagram* [vagrant, but Sir Hugh meant "fragrant"] *posies.*

"*To shallow ...*"

Simple returned and said, "Yonder he is coming this way, Sir Hugh."

"He's welcome," Sir Hugh replied.

Sir Hugh sang this:

"*To shallow rivers, to whose falls —*"

He then said, "Heaven prosper the right! What weapons is he carrying?"

"No weapons, sir, that I could see," Simple said.

He added, "There are also coming my master, Justice Shallow, and another gentleman, from a slightly different direction — from Frogmore, over the stile, this way. They are close by."

"Please, give me my cloak," Sir Hugh said.

Realizing that his arms were occupied with holding a Bible and a sword, he added, "Or else keep it in your arms."

Mr. Page, Justice Shallow, and Slender arrived. Mr. Page and Justice Shallow were going to pretend that they did not know that Sir Hugh and Doctor Caius were supposed to fight a duel.

Justice Shallow said to Sir Hugh, "How are you now, Mr. Parson? Good morning, good Sir Hugh."

He saw the Bible in Sir Hugh's hand and said, "Keep a gamester from the dice, and a good student from his book, and it is wonderful."

Mr. Slender heard the reference to a book and thought, *Ah, sweet Anne Page!* He was imagining that he was in love with Anne Page.

Mr. Page said, "May God save you, good Sir Hugh!"

"God pless you from His mercy sake, all of you!" Sir Hugh replied.

Justice Shallow, noticing the sword that Sir Hugh was holding, said, "What, the sword and the word! Do you study them both, Mr. Parson?"

Mr. Page said, "And you are still youthful! You must be still youthful because you are not wearing a cloak on this raw, cold, rheumatism-causing day!"

"There is reasons and causes for it," Sir Hugh replied.

Mr. Page said, "We have come to you to do a good deed, Mr. Parson."

"Fery [Very] well," Sir Hugh replied. "What is it?"

"Yonder is a most reverend gentleman," Mr. Page said, "who, most likely having received wrong by some person, is at most odds with his own gravity and patience that ever you saw."

Justice Shallow added, "I have lived fourscore years and upward; I never heard a man of his position, gravity, and learning be so wide of his own respect — he has completely lost control of himself."

"Who is he?" Sir Hugh asked.

"I think you know him: Doctor Caius, the renowned French physician," Mr. Page said.

"Got's [God's] will, and His passion of my heart! I had as lief you would tell me of a mess of porridge — I would just as soon hear about a mess of porridge as hear about him!"

"Why?" Mr. Page asked.

Sir Hugh replied, "He has no more knowledge in Hibocrates [Hippocrates] and Galen than a mess of porridge — and he is a knave besides; he is as cowardly a knave as you would desires to be acquainted withal."

Hippocrates, like Galen, was an ancient doctor of medicine. From Hippocrates, we get the Hippocratic Oath.

Mr. Page said to Justice Shallow, "I promise you, he's the man who should fight with him."

In other words, Mr. Page was pretending to just now realize that Sir Hugh and Doctor Caius intended to fight each other. He was saying to the other people that Sir Hugh is the man who should — and intends to — fight Doctor Caius.

Hearing the reference to his rival, Doctor Caius, Slender thought, *Oh, sweet Anne Page!*

Justice Shallow said, "It appears so by his weapons. Keep Sir Hugh and Doctor Caius apart — here comes Doctor Caius."

The Host of the Garter Inn, Doctor Caius, and John Rugby walked up to the group of men.

Mr. Page said to Sir Hugh, "Good Mr. Parson, put away your weapon."

Justice Shallow said to Doctor Caius, "You do the same, good Doctor."

Simple had not noticed that Doctor Caius was carrying a sword.

The Host said, "Disarm both men, and let them talk to each other. Let them keep their limbs whole and hack our English."

"Please," Doctor Caius said to Sir Hugh, "I pray you, let-a me speak a word with your ear. Vherefore vill you not [Why won't you] meet-a me in a duel?"

Sir Hugh whispered to Doctor Caius, "Please, be patient. We will meet soon at a good time."

"By gar, you are de coward, de Jack dog, John ape!"

Doctor Caius was varying the insult of calling someone a jackanape.

Sir Hugh whispered to Doctor Caius, "Please let us not be laughing-stocks for other men's entertainments; I want to be friends with you, and I will one way or other make you amends."

He then said loudly, "I will knog [knock] your urinals about your knave's cockscomb [head] for missing your meetings and appointments."

Doctor Caius said, "*Diable!* [The Devil!] Jack Rugby — mine Host de Jarteer [Garter] — have I not stay [wait] for him to kill him? Have I not, at de place I did appoint?"

Sir Hugh said, "As I am a Christians soul now, look you, this is the place appointed: I'll be judgment [judged] by mine Host of the Garter."

Both men had been misled by the Host of the Garter Inn, who had sent them to different places so that they would not fight each other but could be laughed at.

The Host said, "Peace, I say, Gallia and Gaul, French and Welsh, soul-curer and body-curer!"

Gallia and Gaul both refer to France, but the Host meant for the terms to refer to Wales and France. He should have used "Galles" instead of "Gallia" — "Galles" is the French name for Wales.

Doctor Caius said, "Ay, dat is very good; excellent."

The Host said, "Peace, I say! Be quiet! Listen to the Host of the Garter. Am I politic? Am I subtle? Am I a Machiavel?"

The Host was asking, *Am I sneaky?* The answer could very well rightly be, *Yes.* Machiavelli was the author of *The Prince*, a treatise about political intrigue and how to get power.

The Host did not want either Sir Hugh or Doctor Caius to be hurt in a duel; both provided useful services to the community.

The Host continued, "Shall I lose my doctor? No; he gives me the potions and the motions."

The potions were laxatives, and the motions were the result of the laxatives.

The Host continued, "Shall I lose my parson, my priest, my Sir Hugh? No; he gives me the pro-verbs and the no-verbs."

Pro-verbs, aka proverbs, taught wisdom and what we ought to do; "pro" means "in favor of." No-verbs taught us what not to do: "Thou shalt not...."

The Host said to Doctor Caius, "Give me your hand, terrestrial; good." He then said to Sir Hugh, "Give me your hand, celestial; good."

Then he said to both of them, "Boys of learning, I have deceived you both; I have directed you to different places: Your hearts are mighty, your skins are whole, and let draughts of heated wine sweetened with burnt sugar be the conclusion of your quarrel."

The Host continued, "No one has any need to use these swords. Follow me, lads of peace; follow, follow, follow. Let us go to the Garter Inn."

Justice Shallow said, "Believe me, he is a madcap Host. Follow, gentlemen, follow."

Slender thought, *Oh, sweet Anne Page!*

Justice Shallow, Slender, Mr. Page, and the Host departed, leaving Sir Hugh and Doctor Caius behind. The two men no longer wanted to fight each other, but they were angry about being made laughingstocks.

Doctor Caius said, "Ha, do I perceive dat? Have you — the Host — make-a de sot [fool] of us, ha, ha?"

"This is rich," Sir Hugh said sarcastically. "He has made us his vlouting-stog [flouting-stock, aka laughing-stock]. I desire you that we may be friends; and let us knog our prains together [knock our brains together, aka put our heads together] to be revenge [revenged] on this same scall, scurvy, cogging companion: the Host of the Garter."

Both "scall" and "scurvy" referred to skin diseases. By "cogging companion," Sir Hugh meant "cheating rascal."

Doctor Caius said, "By gar, with all my heart. He promise to bring me [to] where is Anne Page; by gar, he deceive me, too."

"Well, I will smite his noddles [head]. Please, follow me."

Mrs. Page and Robin, Falstaff's page, talked together on a Windsor street. Robin had been walking ahead of Mrs. Page.

"Keep on going, little gallant," Mrs. Page said. "You used to be a follower, but now you are a leader. Which do you prefer? To lead my eyes, or to eye your master's heels?"

Robin replied, "I had rather, truly, to go before you like a man than to follow him like a dwarf."

"You are a flattering boy," Mrs. Page said. "Now I see you'll be a courtier."

Mr. Ford walked up to them and said, "It is good to see you, Mrs. Page. Where are you going?"

"Truly, sir, to see your wife. Is she at home?"

"Yes, and she is as idle as she can be without going to pieces because she lacks company. I think that if your husbands were dead, you two would marry."

"You can sure of that — we would marry two other husbands."

Looking at Robin, who was gaily dressed in eccentric clothing provided to him by Falstaff, Mr. Ford asked, "Where did you get this pretty weather cock?"

"I cannot remember what the dickens his name is from whom my husband got him," Mrs. Page replied.

She asked Robin, "What do you call your knight's name?"

"Sir John Falstaff," Robin replied.

"Sir John Falstaff!" Mr. Ford exclaimed.

"That is the man," Mrs. Page said. "I can never remember his name. There is such a friendship between my good husband and him!"

She asked, "Is your wife really at home?"

"Indeed she is."

"If you don't mind, I will leave now," Mrs. Page said. "I am sick until I see her."

Mrs. Page and Robin departed.

Mr. Ford said to himself, "Has Mr. Page any brains? Has he any eyes? Has he any thinking? Sure, he does, but they sleep; he has no use of them.

"Why, this boy will carry a letter twenty miles as easily as a cannon will shoot point-blank twelve score — two hundred and forty — paces. He indulges his wife's inclination; he gives her folly encouragement and opportunity. And now she's going to my wife, and Falstaff's page is with her. A man may hear this shower sing in the wind — it is obvious what bad thing is going to happen. And Falstaff's page is with her! Good plots, they are laid; and our wives who revolt against their marital vows share damnation together.

"Well, I will catch Falstaff with my wife, then I will torment my wife. I will pluck the borrowed veil of virtue from the only-appears-to-be-virtuous Mrs. Page, I will reveal that Mr. Page himself is an overly confident and perverse Actaeon, aka cuckold; and to these violent proceedings all my neighbors shall be spectators."

A clock struck the hour.

Mr. Ford said to himself, "The clock gives me my cue, and my assurance bids me search my house. There I shall find Falstaff: I shall be rather praised for this than mocked; it is as positive as the earth is firm that Falstaff is there in my house. I will go."

Mr. Page, Justice Shallow, Slender, the Host, Sir Hugh Evans, Doctor Caius, and John Rugby walked up to Mr. Ford and greeted him: "It is good to see you."

"Believe me, this is a good knot — group — of people," Mr. Ford said.

He wanted them to be witnesses to his wife's infidelity, so he said, "I have good cheer — food, drink, and entertainment — at home; and I invite you all to go with me."

Justice Shallow said, "I must excuse myself, Mr. Ford."

Slender added, "And so must I, sir. We have arranged to dine with Miss Anne, and I would not break my promise to her for more money than I'll speak of."

"We have lingered about a match between Anne Page and my cousin Slender, and this day we shall have our answer," Justice Shallow said.

Justice Shallow and Slender lived in Gloucestershire, but they had lingered at Windsor because of hope for a marriage between Slender and Anne Page.

"I hope I have your good will, father Page," Slender said. He hoped that Mr. Page would soon be his father-in-law.

"You have, Mr. Slender," Mr. Page said. "I am entirely for you, and I hope that you will marry my daughter."

He added, "Doctor Caius, my wife is entirely for you and wants our daughter to marry you."

Doctor Caius replied, "Yes, by gar [God]; and de maid [the maiden] is love-a me: my nursh-a [nurse, aka housekeeper] Quickly tell me so mush [much]."

The Host asked Mr. Page, "What do you think about young Mr. Fenton? He capers, he dances, he has the eyes of youth, he writes verses, he speaks holiday words in a pleasing manner, and he smells pleasant like April and May. He will succeed in marrying Anne! He will succeed! It is in his buttons! Underneath those buttons is a male body a young maiden will like! He will succeed!"

"He will not succeed in obtaining my consent to the match, I promise you," Mr. Page said. "The gentleman has no property or income, he kept company with the wild Prince Hal of Wales and with Poins, he is of too high a social status for we middle-class folk, and he knows too much of upper-class people and behavior to fit in with us. No, he shall not knit a knot in his fortunes with the finger of my substance — he will not repair his broken finances with the bandage of my money."

Mr. Page had used an interesting image when he said that "he shall not knit a knot in his fortunes with the finger of my substance." The image was that of a person tying a knot with the help of another person's finger. The first person would tie part of a knot, the second person would place a finger in the right spot to keep the knot from becoming undone, and the first person would tie the rest of the knot.

Mr. Page continued, "If he marries my daughter, then let him marry her without obtaining a dowry. The wealth I have waits on my consent, and my consent goes not Fenton's way."

Mr. Ford said, "I ask you heartily — some of you go home with me to dinner. Besides your food and drink, you shall have entertainment: I will show you a monster."

This got their attention.

He then said, "Doctor Caius, you shall go with me; so shall you, Mr. Page; and so shall you, Sir Hugh."

Justice Shallow said, "Well, fare you well."

He whispered to Slender, "We shall have the freer wooing at Mr. Page's."

Justice Shallow and Slender exited.

Doctor Caius said, "Go home, John Rugby; I will go home soon."

Rugby departed.

The Host said, "Farewell, my hearts. I will go to my honest knight Falstaff, and drink canary wine with him."

Mr. Ford thought, *I think I shall drink some pipe-wine first with him; I'll make him dance.*

Mr. Ford was capable of wit. He was punning on "pipe," a word that could mean a musical instrument or a cask for wine. The Host's reference to canary wine had made that pun occur to Mr. Ford. A "canary" was a type of dance as well as a type of wine. And by making Falstaff dance, Mr. Ford meant that he would beat him — that would make Falstaff dance around to escape the beating.

He said out loud, "Will you come with me, friends?"

They replied, "We will go with you to see this monster."

— 3.3 —

In a room in the Fords' house, Mrs. Ford called for two servants: "John! Robert!"

Mrs. Page said, "Quickly, quickly! Is the buck-basket —"

A buck-basket was a laundry basket. Mrs. Page and Mrs. Ford had plans for it, and Mrs. Page wanted it to be ready.

Mrs. Ford knew what Mrs. Page wanted to know, and so she interrupted, " — it's ready."

She called, "Robert!"

John and Robert entered the room; they were carrying the buck-basket.

Mrs. Page said, "Come, come, come!"

Mrs. Ford said, "Here, set it down."

"Give your men their instructions," Mrs. Page said. "We must be brief. Falstaff is coming soon."

"As I told you before, John and Robert," Mrs. Ford said, "be ready here close by in the brew-house, and when I suddenly call you, come forth, and without any pause or staggering take this buck-basket on your shoulders. Then trudge with it quickly, and carry it among the whitsters — the people who whiten the laundry — in Datchet Meadow, and there empty it in the muddy ditch by the Thames River."

Mrs. Page asked them, "You will do it?"

Mrs. Ford replied for her servants, "I have told them over and over; they lack no orders. They know what to do."

She said to John and Robert, "Go now, and come when you are called."

John and Robert exited.

Mrs. Page said, "Here comes little Robin."

Robin, Falstaff's page, entered the room.

Mrs. Ford said to him, "How are you, my young sparrow-hawk! What news do you bring with you?"

"My master, Sir John, has come in at your back door, Mrs. Ford, and he requests your company."

"You little Jack-a-Lent," Mrs. Page said. "Have you been true to us? You haven't told Falstaff anything, have you?"

A Jack-a-Lent was a gaily dressed puppet that was popular during Lent. Falstaff had dressed his young page in gaily colored clothing.

"I have been true to you," Robin said to Mrs. Page. "My master does not know that you are here, and he has threatened to put me into everlasting liberty if I tell you — Mrs. Page — that he is here, for he swears he'll turn me away and not employ me."

"You are a good boy," Mrs. Page said. "This secrecy of yours shall be a tailor to you and shall make you a new jacket and stockings. I will make you a present of them."

She added, "Now I'll go and hide."

"Do so," Mrs. Ford replied.

She said to Robin, "Go tell your master that I am alone."

Robin departed to carry out his errand.

She then said, "Mrs. Page, remember your cue to come out of your hiding place."

"I will," Mrs. Page said. "If I do not, hiss at me."

She hid.

Mrs. Ford said, "That's done. We will treat this unwholesome humidity — this gross watery pumpkin — the way he ought to be treated; we'll teach him to know the difference between turtledoves and jays."

Turtledoves were famed for their faithfulness to their mates. Jays were brightly colored and so were associated with painted, loose women. Painted women were women who used cosmetics. Loose women were sexually promiscuous women or prostitutes.

Falstaff entered the room and said, "Have I caught you, my heavenly jewel? Why, now let me die because I have lived long enough. This is the achievement of my ambition. Oh, blessed hour!"

Mrs. Ford replied, "Oh, sweet Sir John!"

"Mrs. Ford, I cannot fawn," Falstaff said. "I cannot prate, Mrs. Ford. Now I shall sin by making this wish: I wish that your husband were dead. I'll swear it before the best lord; if your husband were dead, I would make you my lady."

"I your lady, Sir John!" Mrs. Ford said. "Alas, I should be a pitiful lady!"

"Let the court of France show me such another lady as you," Falstaff said. "I see how your eye would emulate the diamond; you have the right arched beauty of the brow that becomes the ship-tire, the tire-valiant, or any tire of

Venetian admittance. You can look good wearing any headdress: a headdress that is shaped like a ship, a headdress that is fanciful, or any headdress that comes from the city of fashion: Venice."

"I wear a plain kerchief, Sir John," Mrs. Ford said. "My brows become nothing else, nor do they look that well on their own."

"By the Lord, you are a traitor to yourself to say so," Falstaff said. "You would make a perfect courtier; and the firm placing of your foot would give an excellent motion to your turning and walking in a half-hooped petticoat. I see what you would be, if Fortune (your foe) were — not Nature — your friend. Nature is your friend and has made you beautiful, but Fortune is your foe and has made you a middle-class wife rather than a great lady. Come, you cannot deny it."

"Believe me, there are no such qualities in me," Mrs. Ford said.

"What made me love you?" Falstaff said. "Those qualities that you deny having. Let that persuade you there's something extraordinary in you. Come, I cannot fawn and say you are this and that, like a many of these lisping hawthorn-buds, who come like women in men's apparel, and smell like Bucklersbury Street in London when it is filled with sweet-smelling herbs for sale. I cannot fawn, but I love you; I love no one but you; and you deserve my love."

"Do not betray me, sir," Mrs. Ford said. "I am afraid that you love Mrs. Page."

"You might as well say that I love to walk by the gate of the Counter, a prison for debtors. The Counter is famous for its reeking stink, and it is as hateful to me as the reek of a lime-kiln."

"Well, Heaven knows how I love you," Mrs. Ford said, "and you shall one day find out how much I love you."

"Keep in that mind," Falstaff said. "I'll deserve it."

"I must tell you that you deserve to find out how much I love you, or else I could not be in that particular frame of mind."

Robin entered the room and said, "Mrs. Ford! Mrs. Ford! Mrs. Page is at the door, sweating and puffing and looking wildly, and she wants to speak with you right away."

"She must not see me," Falstaff said. "I will hide behind this wall hanging."

"Please, do that," Mrs. Ford said. "She is a very tattling woman. If she sees you, she will tell everyone that she saw you here."

Falstaff hid.

Mrs. Page came into the room.

Mrs. Ford said, "What's the matter?"

"Oh, Mrs. Ford, what have you done? You're shamed!" Mrs. Page replied. "You're overthrown! You're undone for ever! You're ruined!"

"What's the matter, good Mrs. Page?"

"How could you, Mrs. Ford! You have an honest man as your husband, and you are giving him such cause to suspect you!"

"What cause is that?"

"What cause to suspect you! You know what cause! I have been much mistaken about you!"

"Why, what's the matter?" Mrs. Ford asked.

"Your husband is coming here, woman, with all the officers in Windsor," Mrs. Page said, "to search for a gentleman who he says is here now in the house by your consent, to take an ill advantage of his absence. Your reputation will be ruined."

"You are wrong, I hope," Mrs. Ford replied.

"I pray to Heaven that it is not true that you have such a man here! But it is very certain that your husband is coming here with half of the citizens of Windsor at his heels to search for such a man," Mrs. Page said. "I have come ahead of him to warn you. If you know that you are innocent, why, I am glad of it; but if you have a lover here, get him out — and quickly. Be not so amazed that it paralyzes you so that you can do nothing; call all your senses to you; defend your reputation, or bid farewell to your good life for ever."

"What shall I do?" Mrs. Ford said. "There is a gentleman here. He is my dear friend; and I fear not my own shame as much as I fear his peril. I would rather have him out of the house than for me to possess a thousand pounds."

"For shame!" Mrs. Page said. "Don't waste time engaging in wishful thinking. Your husband is almost here, so think of some way to get your gentleman friend out of your house. You cannot hide him inside. Oh, how you have deceived me! Look, here is a buck-basket. If your gentleman friend is of any reasonable size, he may hide in the buck-basket, and we can throw dirty linen over him to hide him. Then you can send your two male servants to take the buck-basket to Datchet Meadow as if the linen were going to be washed or whitened."

"He's too big to hide in the buck-basket," Mrs. Ford said. "What shall I do?"

Falstaff came out from his hiding place and said, "Let me see it! Let me see it! Oh, let me see it! I'll fit! I'll fit! Follow your friend's advice! I'll fit!"

Mrs. Page took Falstaff's love letter to her out of her pocket and said, "Sir John Falstaff! Is this your letter, knight?"

She was pretending to wonder why Falstaff was with Mrs. Ford; after all, he had sent a love letter to her: Mrs. Page.

Falstaff whispered to her, "I love you. Help me get away. Let me hide in the buck-basket. I'll never —"

He got in the buck-basket, and the two women started to cover him with dirty linen.

Mrs. Page said to Robin, "Help to cover your master, boy."

She then said, "Call your male servants, Mrs. Ford."

Finally, she said to Falstaff, "You lying knight!"

Mrs. Ford called, "John! Robert!"

The servants entered the room.

She told them, "Go and pick up these clothes here quickly. Where's the cowl-staff — the pole you use to carry the buck-basket?"

One of the servants found the cowl-staff, but he was working too slowly for Mrs. Ford, who told him, "How you dawdle! Carry the clothes to the laundress in Datchet Meadow. Quickly! Quickly!"

Mr. Ford, Mr. Page, Doctor Caius, and Sir Hugh entered the room.

Robin took the opportunity to exit, unnoticed.

Mr. Ford said to his wife, "Please, come near to me. If I suspect you without cause, why then you can make fun of me. Then I will be your laughingstock; I will deserve it."

He said to the servants, "What are you doing? Where are you carrying this buck-basket?"

A servant replied, "To the laundress."

Mrs. Ford said, "Why, what have you to do with where they carry it? Are you now in charge of laundry in this house? Are you now in charge of the buck-basket?"

"Buck! I would I could wash myself of the buck!" Mr. Ford said. He was thinking of a horned deer and the horns of a cuckold. He said, "Buck! Buck! Buck! Yes, buck; I promise you, buck; and of the season, too, it shall appear."

By season, he meant the rutting season, when a buck's antlers were at their largest.

The servants left, carrying Falstaff away in the buck-basket.

Mr. Ford said, "Gentlemen, I dreamed last night; I'll tell you my dream. Here, here, here are my keys. Ascend to my chambers; search, seek, find out. I'll bet that we'll unkennel the fox. Let me stop this exit first."

He locked the door and said, "That's done. Let's see an escape now."

Mr. Page said, "Good Mr. Ford, stay calm. You are growing overexcited. You wrong yourself too much."

"It is true that I am perturbed, Mr. Page," Mr. Ford said. "Up, gentlemen. You shall see some entertainment soon. Follow me, gentlemen."

He left the room.

Sir Hugh said, "This is fery [very] fantastical humors [moods] and jealousies."

"By gar, this is no [not] the fashion of France; it is not jealous [no jealousy is] in France," Doctor Caius said.

"Let us follow Mr. Ford, gentlemen," Mr. Page said. "We will see the result of his search."

Mr. Page, Doctor Caius, and Sir Hugh exited to follow Mr. Ford.

Mrs. Page said, "Is there not a double excellency in this?"

Mrs. Ford replied, "I don't know which pleases me better, that my husband is deceived, or Sir John. My husband is wrong to be jealous, and Falstaff is wrong to think that I love him."

"What a fright Falstaff was in when your husband asked who was in the basket!" Mrs. Page said.

"I am half afraid that Falstaff will have need of washing; I think that he soiled himself," Mrs. Ford said. "Therefore, throwing him into the water will do him a benefit."

"Hang him, dishonest rascal! I wish that all men who do the same thing as Falstaff could suffer the same distress."

"I think my husband has some special reason to suspect that Falstaff was here," Mrs. Ford said, "because I never saw him so gross in his jealousy until now."

"I will lay a plot to see if that is true," Mrs. Page said, "and we will still be able to play more tricks on Falstaff. His dissolute disease will scarcely be cured by this medicine: His being dunked in the water will not stop him from pursuing us."

Mrs. Ford asked, "Shall we send that foolish carrion, Mistress Quickly, to him, and make an excuse for his being thrown into the water; and give him more hope so that we can punish him a second time?"

"We will do it," Mrs. Page said. "Let us send a message to him to meet us tomorrow at eight o'clock in the morning. We will tell him that we want to make amends for what has happened to him."

Mr. Ford, Mr. Page, Doctor Caius, and Sir Hugh entered the room.

Mr. Ford said, "I cannot find him. Maybe the knave bragged about doing something that he could not actually do."

Mrs. Page whispered to Mrs. Ford, "Did you hear that?"

Mrs. Ford said, "You think you are treating me well, Mr. Ford, do you?"

"Yes, I do," he replied. He was still half-suspicious that his wife was unfaithful.

"May Heaven make you better than your thoughts!"

"Amen!" he said.

Mrs. Page said, "You do yourself mighty wrong, Mr. Ford."

"Yes, yes, I must bear it," he replied. He was quickly beginning to realize that he was most likely wrong to suspect his wife of being unfaithful and therefore he had acted badly.

Sir Hugh said, "If there be anypody [anybody] in the house, and in the chambers, and in the coffers, and in the cupboards, may Heaven forgive my sins at the day of judgment!"

"By gar, nor I, too; there is no bodies," Doctor Caius said.

Mr. Page said, "Shame! Shame! Shame on you, Mr. Ford! Are you not ashamed? What spirit, what Devil suggests this delusion? I would not have your distemper of jealousy for the wealth of Windsor Castle. You are acting as if you were mentally unstable."

"This is my fault, Mr. Page. I suffer for it," Mr. Ford replied.

"You suffer for a pad [bad] conscience," Sir Hugh said. "Your wife is as honest a 'omans as I will desires among five thousand, and five hundred, too."

Sir Hugh's lack of facility in English betrayed him here. It sounded as he were desiring Mrs. Ford.

"By gar, I see it is an honest woman," Doctor Caius said.

"Well, I promised you a dinner," Mr. Ford said. "Come, come, walk in the Park with me until dinner is ready."

He added to his wife, "Please, pardon me. Later I will tell you why I have done this."

He then said, "Wife and Mrs. Page, please pardon me; I beg you heartily to pardon me."

Mr. Page said, "Let's walk in the Park and then go in to dinner, but believe me, we'll mock Mr. Ford. I invite you men tomorrow morning to my house to eat breakfast; afterward, we'll go birding together. I have a fine hawk that will scare birds from the bushes. Shall we go birding together?"

"Yes," Mr. Ford said. "I accept your invitation."

"If there is one, I shall make two in the company," Sir Hugh said.

"If dere be one or two, I shall make-a the turd [third]," Doctor Caius said.

"Please, let's all walk in the Park, Mr. Page," Mr. Ford said.

Sir Hugh whispered to Doctor Caius, "Please now, remembrance tomorrow on that lousy knave, the Host."

The two had a plot to wreak on the Host of the Garter Inn the following day.

"Dat is good; by gar, with all my heart!" Doctor Caius said.

"He is a lousy knave, to have his gibes and his mockeries!" Sir Hugh said.

They left to walk in the Park.

Fenton and Anne Page were talking together in front of the Pages' house.

"I see I cannot get your father's respect and friendship," Fenton said. "Therefore, send me no more to talk to him, sweet Nan."

"What shall we do then?" Anne Page replied.

"Why, you must be yourself and act independently of him. He objects that I am too great of birth and my social status is too high to marry you — and he objects that my estate has been devastated by my expenses and so I am seeking to heal my lack of fortune by marrying you and getting access to his wealth through your dowry. Besides these objections to our being married, he lays other objections before me: my past riotous behavior and my wild friends. And he tells me that it is impossible that I should love you except as a way to gain wealth from him."

"Maybe he is telling you the truth."

"No," Fenton said. "May Heaven favor me in the future only if I am speaking the truth to you. I will, however, confess that your father's wealth was the first motive for my wooing you, Anne. Yet, by wooing you, I found you to be of more value than gold coins or wealth in sealed bags, and now I woo you for the wonderful riches of yourself."

"Gentle Mr. Fenton, still seek my father's respect and approval; continue to seek it, sir. If the most humble suit made at the most favorable opportunity cannot get you my father's approval, why then —"

She saw Justice Shallow, Slender, and Mistress Quickly coming and said, "Let's go over here!"

They went a short distance away and talked together quietly.

Justice Shallow said, "Break up the conversation between Fenton and Anne Page, Mistress Quickly. My kinsman Slender shall speak for himself to Anne Page."

"I'll make a shaft or a bolt on it," Slender said. "By God's eyelid, it is worth a try."

Slender was saying that one way or another he would propose to Anne Page. A shaft and a bolt were references to different kinds of arrows. A shaft was a long, thin arrow, while a bolt was shorter and thicker and shot by crossbows.

Justice Shallow said, "Don't be dismayed."

Slender replied, "No, she shall not dismay me. That will not happen, but I am afraid."

Mistress Quickly said to Anne Page, "Mr. Slender would like to speak a word with you."

"I will go to him," she replied.

She whispered to Fenton, "Slender is my father's choice for my future husband. Oh, what a world of vile ill-favored faults looks handsome when it comes with an income of three hundred pounds a year!"

Mistress Quickly asked, "How are you, good Mr. Fenton? Please, may I speak a word with you?"

Justice Shallow said, "Anne Page is coming; go after her, kinsman. Oh, boy, you had a father! If you succeed in catching her, you will be a father!"

"I had a father, Miss Anne," Slender said. "My uncle can tell you good jests about him."

He said to Justice Swallow, "Please, uncle, tell Miss Anne the jest of how my father stole two geese out of a pen, good uncle."

Slender was botching his wooing of Anne.

Justice Shallow said, "Miss Anne, my cousin loves you."

Slender said, "Yes, I do; I love you as well as I love any woman in Gloucestershire."

Slender's comment could be phrased better.

"He will maintain you like a gentlewoman," Justice Shallow said.

"Yes, that I will," Slender said, "come cut and long-tail, under the degree of a squire."

Slender was saying that he would provide for Anne as well as any person, no matter who, could provide for her — provided that they were not too high in rank. The phrase "cut and long-tail" meant "anyone." The literal meaning was dogs with cut, aka docked, tails and dogs with long tails; in other words, all dogs.

Justice Shallow said, "He will make you a hundred and fifty pounds jointure."

This meant that if Slender were to die, Anne, his widow, would receive an income of a hundred and fifty pounds per year.

Anne Page said, "Good Mr. Shallow, let him woo for himself."

Justice Shallow said, "Good idea. I thank you for it; I thank you for that good comfort."

Justice Shallow was pleased that Anne wanted Slender to woo for himself; he regarded that as evidence that Anne was interested in Slender.

Justice Shallow said to Slender, who had stepped away a few paces, "She wants to speaks to you, kinsman. I'll leave you two alone."

Anne said, "Hello, Mr. Slender."

Slender replied, "Hello, good Miss Anne."

"What is your will?"

"My will?" Slender said. "By God's heart, that's a pretty jest indeed! I have not made my will yet, I thank Heaven. I am not such a sickly creature as to need to do that. I give Heaven praise."

"I mean, Mr. Slender, what do you want of me?"

Slender replied, "Truly, for my own part, I want little or nothing of you. Your father and my uncle have made motions."

Slender meant that a marriage proposal had been made, but "motions" was a word that also referred to bowel movements.

Slender continued, "If it should be my luck to marry you, good; if not, may the man who wins you be happy! Your father and my uncle can tell you how things go better than I can; you may ask your father because here he comes."

Mr. and Mrs. Page walked over to the others.

Mr. Page said, "Hello, Mr. Slender. Love him, daughter Anne. Why, look here! What is Mr. Fenton doing here? You wrong me, sir, thus still to haunt my house. I told you, sir, my daughter is disposed of. She is engaged."

"Mr. Page, don't be impatient with me," Fenton replied.

Mrs. Page said, "Good Mr. Fenton, do not visit my daughter."

"She is not a match for you," Mr. Page said. "She will not marry you."

Mr. Page wanted Slender to be his son-in-law.

Fenton said to Mr. Page, "Sir, will you listen to me?"

"No, good Mr. Fenton," he replied.

He then said, "Come, Mr. Shallow; come, son Slender, come in. Knowing my mind and knowing that I do not want you to marry my daughter, you wrong me by coming here, Mr. Fenton."

Mr. Page, Justice Shallow, and Slender went inside the Pages' house.

Mistress Quickly advised Fenton, "Speak to Mrs. Page."

Fenton said, "Good Mrs. Page, because I love your daughter in such a righteous fashion as I do, I must — against all barriers and rebukes, and contrary to good manners — advance the colors of my love as if I were an army mounting an attack. I must not retire; therefore, let me have your good will."

"Good mother," Anne Page said, "do not marry me to yonder fool."

"I do not intend to," Mrs. Page said. "I seek you a better husband than Slender."

Mistress Quickly said, "She wants you to marry my master, Doctor Caius."

"Alas, I would prefer to be buried alive up to my neck in the earth and bowled to death with turnips used as bowling balls!" Anne cried.

"Come, do not make yourself feel bad," Mrs. Page said.

She added, "Good Mr. Fenton, I will not be your friend or your enemy. I will question my daughter about her love for you, and I will take her answers into consideration. Until then, farewell, sir. She must go inside, or her father will be angry."

"Farewell, gentle Mrs. Page; farewell, Nan," Fenton said.

Mrs. Page and Anne went inside the house.

Mistress Quickly said to Fenton, "This — Mrs. Page taking the feelings of her daughter into consideration — is my doing. Said I, 'Will you cast away your child on a fool, and a physician? Look at Mr. Fenton instead.' This change in Mrs. Page is my doing."

"I thank you," Fenton said, "and I ask you, please, to give my sweet Nan this ring sometime tonight. Here's some money for your pains."

"May Heaven send you good fortune!" Mistress Quickly said.

Fenton departed.

Mistress Quickly said to herself, "He has a kind heart. A woman would run through fire and water for such a man with such a kind heart. But yet I wish that my master, Doctor Caius, had Miss Anne to marry; or I wish that Slender had her to marry; or, truly, I wish that Mr. Fenton had her to marry. I will do what I can for all three of them; for so I have promised, and I'll be as good as my word; but speciously [especially] I will do what I can for Mr. Fenton. Well, I must go on another errand to Sir John Falstaff from my two mistresses: Mrs. Ford and Mrs. Page. What a beast am I to slack on doing my errand!"

The following morning, Falstaff was in a room in the Garter Inn. He was still recovering from having been dumped into the cold water of the Thames River. With him was Bardolph, now a bartender at the Garter.

Falstaff said, "Bardolph, I say —"

"Here I am, sir."

"Go fetch me a quart of wine; put a piece of toast in it."

Bardolph departed to get the wine and toast.

Falstaff said to himself, "Have I lived to be carried in a basket, like a barrowful of butcher's offal, and to be thrown in the Thames? Well, if I am served such another trick, I'll have my brains taken out and buttered, and I will give them to a dog for a new-year's gift. Buttered brains are foolish brains. The rogues slighted me into the river with as little remorse as they would have drowned the blind puppies of a bitch, fifteen in the litter, and you may know by my size that I have a kind of alacrity in sinking; if the bottom were as deep as Hell, I should go all the way down. I would have been drowned, except that the shore was shelvy and shallow. Drowning is a death that I abhor; for the water swells a man; and what a thing should I have been when I had been swelled! I should have been a mountain of mummy — of dead, swollen flesh."

Bardolph returned with the wine and toast.

He said, "Mistress Quickly, sir, is here to speak with you."

"Let me pour in some wine to mix with the Thames water I swallowed last night; for my belly's as cold as if I had swallowed snowballs for pills to cool the reins of my lust. Call her in."

Bardolph called, "Come in, woman!"

As Bardolph was calling for Mistress Quickly, Falstaff drank the quart of wine.

Mistress Quickly entered the room and said, "By your leave, sir. I beg your pardon. I wish your worship a good morning."

"Take away these chalices," Falstaff said to Bardolph. "Go brew me a pottle of sack finely."

The chalices were not used in religious services; they were simply small glasses. Falstaff, a big drinker of wine, wanted Bardolph to bring him a pottle — a half-gallon — of wine.

"With eggs in it, sir?" Bardolph asked.

"Just the wine itself," Falstaff said. "I'll have no pullet-sperm in my brewage."

A pullet is a chicken.

Bardolph exited, and Falstaff said to Mistress Quickly, "Hello!"

"Sir, I come to your worship from Mrs. Ford."

"Mrs. Ford! I have had ford enough; I was thrown into the ford; I have my belly full of ford."

"Alas the day!" Mistress Quickly said. "Good heart, that was not her fault. She does so scold her men-servants; they mistook their erection."

Mistress Quickly meant directions or instructions, not erection, but Falstaff replied, "So did I mine, to build upon a foolish woman's promise. I never should have believed a foolish woman."

"Well, she laments, sir, for what happened. It would yearn [Mistress Quickly meant 'grieve'] your heart to see it. Her husband goes this morning a-birding away from home; she desires you once more to come to her between eight and nine. I must carry a message from you to her quickly. She will make you amends, I promise you."

"Well, I will come and visit her," Falstaff said. "Tell her so; and tell her to think about what a man is: Let her consider his frailty, and then judge of my merit."

Falstaff meant that he was showing merit by being persistent: He was not easily giving up his attempt to commit adultery with Mrs. Ford.

"I will tell her," Mistress Quickly said.

"Do so. Between nine and ten, did you say?"

"Eight and nine, sir."

"Well, go to her," Falstaff said. "I will not miss my meeting with her."

"Peace be with you, sir."

Mistress Quickly exited.

Falstaff said to himself, "I marvel that I have not heard from Mr. Brook; he sent me word to stay within the inn until he came. I like his money well. Oh, here he comes."

Mr. Ford, disguised as Mr. Brook, entered the room.

"Bless you, sir!" Mr. Ford said.

"Hello, Mr. Brook, have you come to know what has happened between me and Ford's wife?"

"That, indeed, Sir John, is my business here."

"Mr. Brook, I will not lie to you. I was at her house the hour she asked me to come."

"How did you do, sir?"

"Very badly, Mr. Brook."

"Why? Did she change her mind?"

"No, Mr. Brook; but the prying cuckold who is her husband, Mr. Brook, dwelling in a continual alarm of jealousy, came in during our encounter, after we had embraced, kissed, confessed our love for each other, and, as it were, spoke the prologue of our comedy."

Falstaff was exaggerating his "success" with Mrs. Ford.

He continued, "Indeed, at the heels of Mr. Brook came a rabble of his companions, thither provoked and instigated by his ill temper to search his house for his wife's love."

"What, while you were there?" the disguised Mr. Ford said.

"Yes, while I was there."

"And did he search for you, and could not find you?"

"You shall hear the story," Falstaff said. "As good luck would have it, Mrs. Page came in and told us that Ford was coming, and as a result of her cunning and Ford's wife's distraction, they put me in a buck-basket and Mrs. Ford's servants carried me away from the house."

"A buck-basket!"

"By the Lord, a buck-basket! They rammed me in with foul and dirty shirts and smocks, socks, foul stockings, and greasy handkerchiefs; Mr. Brook, there was the rankest collection of dirty clothing with the most villainous smell that ever offended nostril."

"And how long did you lie there?"

"I will tell you, Mr. Brook, what I have suffered in my attempt to bring this woman to do evil for your benefit. After I was thus crammed in the basket, a couple of Ford's knaves, aka his hinds and his servants, were ordered by Mrs. Ford to carry me in the name of foul clothes to Datchet Lane, the lane that leads to Datchet Meadow. They took me on their shoulders and met the jealous knave their master in the doorway. He asked them once or twice what they had in their basket. I quaked for fear that the lunatic knave would have searched the basket; but fate, ordaining that Ford should be a cuckold, held his hand. Well, he continued on into the house to search it, and away went I with the foul clothes.

"But consider what happened next, Mr. Brook. I suffered the pangs of three different possible deaths. First, I could have died from an intolerable fright; I was afraid that I would be detected by a jealous rotten bellwether ram with a bell around its neck that leads the flock.

"Second, I had to bend, like a good bilbo sword, in the circumference of a peck, hilt to point, heel to head, in order to fit into the basket."

Good swords could be bent without breaking. A sword from Bilbao, Spain, was tested for excellence by bending it from tip to hilt. If it did not break, it was a good sword. A peck is a quarter of a bushel; Sir Falstaff was complaining about his bulk being squeezed into a very small space.

Falstaff continued, "Third, I was stuffed in that basket like a strongly smelling distilled liquid in a glass container. And in that basket were stinking clothes that fermented in their own grease. Think of that — a man of my nature — think of that — who is as subject to heat as butter; I am a man of continual dissolving and thaw. I melt in heat like butter. It was a miracle that I escaped suffocation.

"And in the height of this bath, when I was more than half stewed in grease, like a Dutch dish cooked with too much butter, I was then thrown into the Thames River, and glowing hot, I was cooled in that surge of cold water like a glowing-hot horseshoe thrown into water. Think of that — I was hissing hot — think of that, Mr. Brook."

"In all seriousness," Mr. Ford said, "I am sorry that for my sake you have suffered all this. My suit then is desperate; I assume that you will no longer try to seduce Mrs. Ford?"

"Mr. Brook, I will be thrown into the volcano Etna, as I have been into the Thames River, before I will stop trying to seduce her. Her husband is this morning gone hunting birds, and I have received from her another time to meet her. Between eight and nine is the hour, Mr. Brook."

"It is already past eight, sir," Mr. Ford said.

"Is it? I will then go to my appointment," Falstaff said. "Come to me at your convenient leisure, and you shall know how I succeed; and the conclusion shall be crowned with your enjoying her. *Adieu*. You shall have her, Mr. Brook; Mr. Brook, you shall cuckold Ford."

Falstaff exited.

"Hmm!" Mr. Ford said to himself, "Is this a vision? Is this a dream? Do I sleep? Mr. Ford, wake up! Wake up, Mr. Ford! There's a hole made in your best coat, Mr. Ford. Mr. Ford, you have a fault. This is what it is to be married! This is what it is to have linen and buck-baskets! Well, I will proclaim myself what I am."

Mr. Ford meant that he was a cuckold.

He continued, "I will now surprise Falstaff, the lecher. He is at my house. He cannot escape me; it is impossible for him to escape from me this time. He cannot creep into a purse that holds small coins, nor into a pepper shaker. However, in case the Devil who guides him should aid him, I will search impossible places. Though what I am I cannot avoid, yet to be what I would not shall not make me tame. If I have horns to make me mad, then let the proverb go with me: I'll be horn-mad."

Mr. Ford thought that he was a cuckold, but he did not want to say the word, and so he said phrases such as "Though what I am I cannot avoid" and "yet to be what I would not."

CHAPTER 4
— 4.1 —

On a public street stood Mrs. Page, Mistress Quickly, and William Page, the Pages' young son, who was studying Latin, as even very young pupils did at that time.

Speaking about Falstaff, Mrs. Page asked Mistress Quickly, "Do you think that he is already at Mrs. Ford's house?"

"I am sure that he is by this time, or will be immediately, but, truly, he is very outrageously angry about being thrown into the water. Mrs. Ford wants you to go to her right away."

Mrs. Page replied, "I'll be with her very soon; first I need to take my young man here to school."

She looked up and said, "Look, his schoolmaster — Sir Hugh — is coming; I see that today is a playing day — a holiday from school."

Because Sir Hugh was a university-educated priest, he was the schoolmaster in Windsor.

She said, "How are you, Sir Hugh? Is there no school today?"

"No, there is no school," Sir Hugh replied. "Mr. Slender has requested that I allow the boys to play today."

"God bless him," Mistress Quickly said.

Mrs. Page said, "Sir Hugh, my husband says my son is not learning anything at all in school. Please, ask him some questions about his knowledge of Latin."

"Come here, William," Sir Hugh said. "Hold up your head; come here."

"Come on, son," Mrs. Page said. "Hold up your head; answer your teacher, and don't be afraid."

With his Welsh accent, Sir Hugh asked, "William, how many numbers is in nouns?"

"Two."

William was correct: the two numbers were singular and plural.

Latin is a language that has inflections according to number and case. The inflections are changes in the form of the word that reveal information such as whether the noun is singular or plural. The inflections also reveal whether a noun is in the nominative, genitive, accusative, ablative, or vocative case.

Mistress Quickly, who knew no Latin, said, "Truly, I thought there had been one number more because they say, 'God's nouns.'"

She was mistaken. People sometimes referred to God's 'ounds, or wounds, not God's nouns. Also, Jesus suffered five wounds on the cross, not three. He was wounded in his side, his hands, and his feet.

"Peace your tattlings!" Sir Hugh said to Mistress Quickly; he meant, "Be quiet!"

He then asked, "What is 'fair,' William?"

William gave the Latin word for "fair," aka "beautiful": "*Pulcher*."

Mistress Quickly misunderstood: "Polecats! There are fairer things than polecats, surely."

Polecats were regarded as vermin; in addition, the word "polecat" was a slang term for a prostitute.

"You are a very simplicity 'oman [simple-minded woman]," Sir Hugh said to her. "Please, be quiet."

He then asked, "What is *lapis*, William?"

William correctly translated the Latin word "*lapis*": "A stone."

"And what is 'a stone,' William?"

"A pebble."

Here, William answered incorrectly. Sir Hugh had wanted William to translate the English word "stone" into Latin.

Sir Hugh said, "No, it is *lapis*. Please, remember in your prain [brain]."

William said, "*Lapis*."

"That is a good William," Sir Hugh said. "What is he, William, who does lend articles?"

Articles are words such as "this" and "that."

William had memorized the answer from his Latin book and quoted it word for word: "Articles are borrowed of the pronoun, and be thus declined, *Singulariter, nominativo, hic, haec, hoc*."

Singulariter means "in the singular," *nominativo* means "in the nominative case."

Hic, haec, hoc are all Latin words meaning "this." *Hic* is masculine; *haec* is feminine; and *hoc* is neuter.

Sir Hugh said in his Welsh accent, "*Nominativo, hig, hag, hog*. Please, listen: *genitivo, hujus*. Well, what is your accusative case?"

Genitivo means "in the genitive case; *hujus* means "of this."

William replied, "*Accusativo, hinc.*"

Accusativo means "in the accusative case." However, William erred when he answered *hinc*; he should have answered *hunc*.

Sir Hugh corrected him: "Please, have your remembrance, child, accusative, *hung, hang, hog* [*hunc, hanc, hoc*]."

Mistress Quickly said, "'Hang-hog' is Latin for bacon, I bet."

Bacon is hung and then smoked and preserved. A story was told about a prisoner named Hog who once tried to get out of being hung by saying that he was related to a VIP named Sir Nicholas Bacon, who replied that the prisoner and he could not be related unless the prisoner was hanged because Hog does not become Bacon until it is hanged.

Sir Hugh said, "Leave your prabbles [prattling brabbles, aka trivial words], 'oman."

He then asked, "What is the *focative* case, William?"

By "the *focative* case," Sir Hugh meant "the vocative case."

"O — *vocativo*, O," William replied. In a way, William was correct. When you address someone by name in Latin, you are using the vocative case.

This is a translation of a name in the vocative case from Latin to English: "Oh, William."

Sir Hugh said, "Remember, William; *focative* is *caret*."

Caret is Latin for "It is lacking." Sir Hugh meant that although names can be in the vocative case, the articles *hic, haec, hoc* lack a vocative case.

Mistress Quickly, who heard the Latin word "*caret*" but understood it to be the English word "carrot," said, "And that's a good root."

Anyone with a bawdy sense of humor who heard the conversation could have had a good laugh. Sir Hugh's pronunciation of *focative* called to mind a four-letter English word that began with *f* and ended with *k*. An "O" was a letter that was then used to refer to a vagina. And "carrot" was a word then used to refer to a penis.

Sir Hugh said to Mistress Quickly, "Stop speaking, 'oman."

Mrs. Page added, "Quiet!"

Sir Hugh asked, "What is your genitive case plural, William?"

"Genitive case?" William asked.

"Yes."

William answered, "Genitive — *horum, harum, horum*."

He had answered correctly, but Mistress Quickly, who knew no Latin, was shocked. She understood "genitive case" to mean "Jenny's case." Prostitutes were called by diminutive names such as Jenny, and the word "case" was then used to refer to a vagina. In addition, she heard the Latin word "*horum*" and thought that she was hearing the English word "whore."

Mistress Quickly said, "God's vengeance on Jenny's case! Darn her! Never say her name, child, if she is a whore."

Sir Hugh said, "For shame, 'oman."

Mistress Quickly defended herself: "You do ill to teach the child such words."

She said to Mrs. Page, "He teaches him to hick and to hack, which they'll do fast enough by themselves."

To "hick" is to hiccup after drinking excessively, and to "hack" is to fornicate.

Mistress Quickly said to Sir Hugh, "And to say the word *horum*! Shame on you!"

Sir Hugh replied, "Are you lunatics, 'oman? Have you no understandings for your cases and the numbers of the genders? You are as foolish Christian creatures as I would desires."

"Please, be quiet," Mrs. Page said to Mistress Quickly.

Sir Hugh said, "Show me now, William, some declensions of your pronouns."

"I have forgotten that," William said.

"It is *qui, quae, quod*," Sir Hugh said. "If you forget your *quie*s, your *quae*s, and your *quod*s, you must be preeches."

By "preeches," Sir Hugh meant "breeched" — William would be spanked after his britches were pulled down.

Sir Hugh then said to William, "Go your ways, and play; go."

"He is a better scholar than I thought he was," Mrs. Page said.

"He is a good sprag [alert, clever] memory," Sir Hugh said. "Farewell, Mrs. Page."

"*Adieu*, good Sir Hugh."

Sir Hugh departed.

Mrs. Page said to her son, "Let's go home, boy. Come, we stay here too long."

Falstaff and Mrs. Ford were speaking in a room in the Fords' house.

Falstaff said, "Mrs. Ford, your sorrow has eaten up and taken away my suffering. I see that you return my love, and I declare to you that I match your love exactly — not only, Mrs. Ford, in the simple act and office of love, but in everything that accompanies it — the proper apparel, accompaniment, and ceremony. But are you sure that your husband is away now?"

"He's hunting birds, sweet Sir John," Mrs. Ford said.

Outside the house, Mrs. Page called, "Hello, friend! Are you home?"

Mrs. Ford said, "Step into this room and stay out of sight, Sir John."

Falstaff went into the other room.

Mrs. Page entered the house and said, "How are you now, sweetheart? Who's at home besides yourself?"

"Why, no one but my own servants."

"Indeed!"

"I have told you the truth," Mrs. Ford said.

She whispered to Mrs. Page, "Speak louder so that Falstaff can hear you."

"Truly," Mrs. Page replied, speaking loudly, "I am so glad you have nobody else here."

"Why?"

"Why, woman, your husband is in his old lunatic mind again," Mrs. Page replied. "He so takes on yonder with my husband; he so rails against all married mankind, he so curses all Eve's daughters of whatsoever temperament, and he so hits himself on the forehead, crying, 'Show yourself! Show yourself!' that any madness I have ever before beheld in him now seems only tameness, civility, and patience compared to this distemper he is in now."

When Mr. Ford hit his forehead and yelled, "Show yourself! Show yourself!" he was referring to the metaphorical cuckold's horns that he felt that his wife had given to him.

Mrs. Page said, "I am glad the fat knight is not here."

"Why, does my husband talk about Falstaff?" Mrs. Ford asked.

"He talks about no one but him; and he swears that Falstaff was carried out of your house in a basket the last time he searched for him. He protests to my husband that Falstaff is now here, and he has drawn my husband and the rest of their company from their hunting of birds to see whether his suspicion is correct. I am glad that the knight is not here; now your husband shall see how foolish his suspicions are."

"How near is my husband, Mrs. Page?"

"Very near. He is at the end of the street. He will be here almost immediately."

"I am ruined!" Mrs. Ford said. "The knight is here."

"Why, then you are utterly shamed, and he will soon be a dead man. What a woman are you! Send him away! Send him away! Better shame than murder! You will be shamed, but if he escapes, he will avoid being murdered!"

"How can he get out of here? How can I hide him? Shall I put him into the buck-basket again?"

Falstaff came out of hiding and said, "No, I will not hide again in the basket. Can't I leave before he arrives here?"

Mrs. Page said, "No. Alas, three of Mr. Ford's brothers are watching the door. They are carrying pistols so that no one can go out the door; otherwise, you might slip away before he came. But what are you doing here?"

Ignoring that question, Falstaff said, "What shall I do? I know. I'll creep up into the chimney."

Mrs. Ford said, "Mr. Ford and his hunting partners always fire their birding guns up the chimney. It is a safe way to ensure that they are not loaded. I know where you can hide: Creep into the kiln."

The kiln was where the cooking took place.

"Where is it?" Falstaff asked.

"My husband will look there, I swear," Mrs. Ford said. "He will look everywhere: cupboards, coffers, chests, trunks, wells, vaults. He knows all the places where a man can hide, and he will search all of them. Falstaff, you cannot hide in this house."

"I'll go out of the house then."

"If you go out of this house, you die, Sir John," Mrs. Page said. "Unless you go out disguised —"

"How can we disguise him?" Mrs. Ford asked.

"I don't know!" Mrs. Page said. "There is no woman's gown big enough for him to put on as a disguise; otherwise, he might put on a hat, a muffler around his throat, and a kerchief on his head under his hat, and so escape."

"Good hearts, devise some kind of disguise," Falstaff said. "Better an inconvenience rather than a calamity."

"My maid's aunt, the fat woman of Brentford, has a dress upstairs," Mrs. Ford said.

"I give my word that the dress will fit him," Mrs. Page said. "She's as big as he is: and there's her fringed hat and her muffler, too. Run upstairs and put on her dress, Sir John."

"Go, go, sweet Sir John. Mrs. Page and I will look for a kerchief you can put on your head."

"Quickly, quickly!" Mrs. Page said. "We'll come and help disguise you very soon. In the meanwhile, put on the dress."

Falstaff went upstairs to put on the dress.

"I wish that my husband would see Falstaff in this disguise," Mrs. Ford said. "He cannot abide the old woman of Brentford; he swears that she's a witch and he has forbidden her to enter my house and has threatened to beat her."

"May Heaven guide Falstaff to your husband's cudgel, and may the Devil guide his cudgel afterwards!"

"But is my husband really coming?"

"In all seriousness, yes," Mrs. Page said, "and he talks about the buck-basket, too, but I do not know how he learned about that."

"We'll make use of the buck-basket again," Mrs. Ford said. "I'll tell my manservants to carry the buck-basket again so that they will meet my husband at the door with it, as they did last time."

"Your husband will be here very soon," Mrs. Page said. "Let's go dress Falstaff like the witch of Brentford."

"I'll first give my manservants orders about what they shall do with the buck-basket. Go up to Falstaff; I'll bring him a kerchief for his head very quickly."

Mrs. Ford departed.

Mrs. Page said to herself, "Hang Falstaff, that dishonest varlet! We cannot treat him badly enough. We'll leave a proof, by that which we will do, that wives may be merry, and yet be honest, too. We do not commit adultery although we often jest and laugh. Remember the old, but true, proverb: Quiet swine eat all the pigswill. The pig that is quiet is the one that is actually feeding."

She went upstairs.

Mrs. Ford came back with two manservants.

"Go, sirs, take the buck-basket again on your shoulders. Your master is almost at the door; if he orders you to set it down, obey him. Quickly, do it."

She went upstairs.

The first manservant said, "Come, come, lift it up."

The second manservant said, "Pray to Heaven that it is not full of knight again."

"I hope that it is not," the first manservant said. "I would rather carry a buck-basket filled with lead."

Mr. Ford, Mr. Page, Justice Shallow, Doctor Caius, and Sir Hugh entered the room.

Mr. Ford said, "If my suspicions prove to be wrong, I will look like a fool, true. But if my suspicions prove to be true and I allow my wife to commit adultery through my negligence, do you have any way to make me not a fool again?"

Mr. Ford ordered the manservants, "Set down the basket, villains! Somebody call my wife. Is there a youth — a fortunate lover — in this buck-basket? Oh, you panderly rascals — you act like panders! There's a knot of men, a gang, a pack, a conspiracy against me. Now shall the truth be revealed and the Devil shamed. Remember this proverb: Tell the truth and shame the Devil!"

No one had called his wife, so Mr. Ford did it: "Hello, wife, I say! Come, come here! Look at these honest clothes you sent forth to be bleached!"

Mr. Page said, "Why, this surpasses belief, Mr. Ford; this is incredible. You ought not to be allowed loose any longer; you ought to be tied up like a madman."

"Why, this is lunatics!" Sir Hugh said. "This is as mad as a mad dog!"

Justice Shallow said, "Indeed, Mr. Ford, this is not well, indeed."

"I agree, sir," Mr. Ford replied.

Mrs. Ford entered the room.

Mr. Ford said, "Come here, Mrs. Ford: Mrs. Ford the honest and faithful woman, the modest wife, the virtuous creature, who has a jealous fool for her husband! I suspect without cause, Mrs. Ford, do I?"

"Heaven be my witness that you do," Mrs. Ford said, "if you suspect me in any dishonesty and if you suspect that I have been unfaithful to you in any way."

"Well said, brazen-face!" Mr. Ford said. "Keep it up."

He then started pulling clothing out of the buck-bucket as he said, "Come out of there, damn you!"

"This surpasses everything!" Mr. Page said.

"Are you not ashamed?" Mrs. Ford said. "Let the clothes alone!"

"I shall find you," Mr. Ford said as he searched the basket.

"It is unreasonable!" Sir Hugh said. "Will you take up your wife's clothes? Come away."

Sir Hugh was being unintentionally bawdy. Someone with an indelicate sense of humor could interpret Sir Hugh's words as asking, "Will you take up your wife's dress so you can have sex with her?"

"Empty the basket, I say!" Mr. Ford ordered.

"Why, man, why?" Mrs. Ford asked.

"Mr. Page, as I am a man, I swear that a man was conveyed out of my house yesterday in this buck-basket. Why may he not be there again? I am sure that he is somewhere in my house. My source of information is true; my jealousy is reasonable."

He ordered again, "Pull all the clothing out of the buck-basket."

"If you find a man there, he shall die a flea's death," Mrs. Ford said. "He will have to be as small as a flea to hide there, and I shall squish him between my forefinger and my thumb."

"No man is hiding in that basket," Mr. Page said.

"By my fidelity [faith], this is not well, Mr. Ford," Justice Shallow said. "This disgraces you."

Sir Hugh said, "Mr. Ford, you must pray, and not follow the imaginations of your own heart: This is jealousies."

"Well, the man I am looking for is not here in the buck-basket," Mr. Ford said.

"No, nor anywhere else but in your brain," Mr. Page said.

"Help me to search my house one more time," Mr. Ford said. "If I do not find what I am seeking, suggest no excuse for my extreme behavior, but instead joke about me at your dinner-table. Let everyone use me in comparisons: 'As jealous as Ford, who searched inside a hollow walnut for his wife's lover.' Help me once more; once more search my house with me."

Mrs. Ford called upstairs, "Mrs. Page! You and the old woman come downstairs; my husband will come into the bedchamber."

"Old woman!" Mr. Ford said. "What old woman is that?"

"She is my maid's aunt of Brentford."

"She is a witch, a hussy, an old and cheating hussy! Haven't I forbid her to enter my house? She comes on errands, does she? We are simple men; we do not know what's brought to pass in the name of fortune telling. She works by charms, by spells, by the figure — wax effigies, pentagrams, and astrological horoscopes — and other such pretenses that are beyond our understanding and about which we know nothing!"

He called, "Come down, you witch, you hag, you; come down here, I say!"

"No, please, good, sweet husband!" Mrs. Ford said.

She added, "Good gentlemen, don't allow him to strike the old woman."

Falstaff, now dressed in women's clothing, and Mrs. Page entered the room.

Mrs. Page said, "Come, Mother Prat; come, give me your hand."

"I'll prat her," Mrs. Ford said.

He hit Falstaff several times and yelled, "Out of my door, you witch, you hag, you baggage, you polecat, you bad woman! Out, out! I'll conjure you, I'll fortune-tell you."

Falstaff ran out the door.

"Are you not ashamed?" Mrs. Page said. "I think you have killed the poor woman."

Mrs. Ford said, "He is willing to kill her."

She said sarcastically to her husband, "You ought to be proud of yourself."

"Hang her, the witch!" Mr. Ford said.

"By the yea and no, I think the 'oman is a witch indeed," Sir Hugh said. "I like not when a 'oman has a great peard [beard]; I spy a great peard [beard] under his muffler. Witches have peards."

"Will you follow me, gentlemen?" Mr. Ford asked. "I ask you to please follow me. See if my jealousy has a cause. If I am crying 'Wolf' falsely now, then do not listen to me if I ever cry 'Wolf' again."

"Let's humor him a little further," Mr. Page said. "Come, gentlemen."

Mr. Ford, Mr. Page, Justice Shallow, Doctor Caius, and Sir Hugh went upstairs.

Mrs. Page said, "Believe me, your husband beat Falstaff most pitifully."

Mrs. Ford replied, "No, I swear by the Mass that he did not — he beat him most unpitifully, I believe."

"I'll have the cudgel he used hallowed — sanctified — and hung over the altar," Mrs. Page said. "It has done meritorious service."

"What do you think?" Mrs. Ford asked. "May we, with the warrant of womanhood and the witness of a good conscience, pursue Falstaff with any further revenge? Are we justified in punishing him further?"

"The spirit of wantonness is, I am sure, scared out of him," Mrs. Page said. "Unless the Devil completely owns him with no possibility of redemption, Falstaff will never again, I think, seek to sully us by attempting to commit adultery with us."

"Shall we tell our husbands how we have tricked and punished Falstaff?" Mrs. Ford asked.

"Yes, by all means; if for no other reason than to scrape the jealous imaginings out of your husband's brains. If they can find in their hearts that the poor unvirtuous fat knight should be any further afflicted, the two of us will continue to administer justice to him."

"I'll bet that they will have him publicly shamed," Mrs. Ford said. "I think that would be the best and most fitting conclusion to the jest. Falstaff deserves to be publicly shamed."

"Come, let us go to the forge then and shape our next plan for revenge," Mrs. Page said. "I would not have things cool."

In a room of the Garter Inn, Bardolph said to the Host, "Sir, the Germans desire to have the use of three of your horses: The Duke himself will be tomorrow at the court, and they are going to meet him."

"What Duke is he who is coming so secretly?" the Host said. "I have heard nothing about a Duke being at the court tomorrow. Let me speak with the gentlemen. Do they speak English?"

"Yes, sir," Bardolph said. "I'll call them to come and speak to you."

"They shall use my horses," the Host said, "but I'll make them pay; I'll sauce them and charge them a lot. They reserved rooms at my inn for a week, and I have turned away other guests. They must pay a lot; I'll overcharge them. Come with me."

Mr. and Mrs. Page, Mr. and Mrs. Ford, and Sir Hugh were talking together in a room in the Fords' house. Mrs. Ford and Mrs. Page had shown their husbands the letters that Falstaff had written to them.

"It is one of the best discretions of a 'oman as ever I did look upon," Sir Hugh said.

He meant that Mrs. Ford was one of the most sensible and discreet women that he had ever seen.

Mr. Page asked, "And did he send you both these letters at the same time?"

Mrs. Page replied, "Within a quarter of an hour."

"Pardon me, wife," Mr. Ford said. "Henceforth do what you will; I will suspect the Sun of being cold before I will suspect you of being wanton and unfaithful. Now my honor stands in me as firm as faith, although recently I was a heretic."

"This is good," Mr. Page said. "This is good, but no more, please. Be not as extreme in apologizing for an offense as you were in committing the offense.

"But let our plot go forward. Let our wives once more, to make public entertainment for us, appoint a meeting with this old fat fellow at a place where we may find him and disgrace him for what he has wanted to do."

"There is no better way or plan than the one they spoke of," Mr. Ford said.

"I don't know," Mr. Page said. "They will send him word that they'll meet him in the park at midnight? Nonsense! He'll never come."

"You say he has been thrown in the rivers and has been grievously peaten [beaten] as an old 'oman," Sir Hugh said. "I think there should be terrors in him that he should not come; methinks that since his flesh is punished, he shall have no desires to come."

"I think so, too," Mr. Page said.

"Plan how you'll treat Falstaff when he comes," Mrs. Ford said, "and let us two devise how to bring him there."

Mrs. Page said, "There is an old tale that Herne the Hunter, who was once a forester here in Windsor Forest, all throughout the winter, at midnight, walks round about an oak while wearing great jagged horns, and there he blights the tree and takes the cattle and makes milk cows yield blood and shakes a chain in a most hideous and dreadful manner.

"You have heard of such a spirit, and well you know the superstitious idle-headed elders of long ago learned and passed down to our times this tale of Herne the Hunter as a true tale."

"Why, even now many people are afraid in the deep of night to walk by Herne's Oak," Mr. Page said. "But what about this?"

"We have a plan," Mrs. Ford said. "We want to entice Falstaff to meet us at that oak. He will be disguised as Herne and have huge horns on his head."

"Well, let us suppose that he shows up," Mr. Page said. "Let us also suppose that he is disguised as Herne the Hunter with horns on his head. Once he is there, what shall be done with and to him? What is your plot?"

"We have thought about that, too," Mrs. Page said. "Nan Page my daughter and my little son and three or four more of their age and size we'll dress like elves, the children of elves, and fairies with rounds of waxen candles on their heads, and rattles in their hands. Suddenly, as Falstaff, Mrs. Ford, and I are newly met, let them come out of a sawpit where timber is sawed and rush at us as they sing some wild and confused song. When we see them, Mrs. Ford and I in great amazedness will run away. Then they will all encircle him round about and, fairy-like, pinch the unclean knight, and ask him why, at that hour of fairy revel, in their so sacred paths he dares to tread in such a profane shape."

"And until he tells the truth," Mrs. Ford said, "the pretend fairies will pinch him without stopping and burn him with their candles."

"Once the truth is known," Mrs. Page said, "we'll all present ourselves, take off his horns, and laugh at him all the way back home to Windsor."

Mr. Ford said, "The children must be taught well how to do this, and they must practice, or they won't be able to do it."

"I will teach the children their behaviors," Sir Hugh said, "and I will be like a jack-an-apes — an evil spirit — also, to burn the knight with my candle."

"That will be excellent," Mr. Ford said. "I'll go and buy them masks."

Mrs. Page said, "My Nan shall be the Fairy Queen, and she will be finely attired in a robe of white."

"I will go and buy white silk," Mr. Page said.

He thought, *I also have formed a plan. During the night, Mr. Slender will steal away with Nan, my daughter, and take her to the nearby village of Eton and marry her.*

He said out loud, "Send a message to Falstaff right away."

Mr. Ford said, "I will disguise myself again as Brook and go to him. He will tell me what he intends to do. I am sure that he will come."

"Don't you worry about that," Mrs. Page said. "Go and get us everything we need for our fairies."

"Let us get going," Sir Hugh said. "It is admirable pleasures and fery [very] honest knaveries."

Mr. Page, Mr. Ford, and Sir Hugh exited.

Mrs. Page said, "Go, Mrs. Ford. Send a message quickly to Sir John, so that we know what he plans to do."

Mrs. Ford exited.

Mrs. Page said to herself, "I'll go to Doctor Caius. He has my good will, and I want no one but him to marry my daughter, Nan Page. That Slender, although he owns lots of land, is an idiot; my husband likes Slender best of all my daughter's suitors.

"Doctor Caius is well moneyed, and his friends are powerful at court. He, none but he, shall marry my daughter even though twenty thousand men worthier than him should want to marry her."

In a room in the Garter Inn, the Host was talking with Simple, Slender's servant. The Host was in a good mood and using extravagant language. He was also willing to have fun at the expense of Simple.

"What would you have, boor?" the Host asked. "What, thick-skin! Speak, breathe, discuss; brief, short, quick, snap."

"Sir, I have come to speak with Sir John Falstaff," Simple said. "Master Slender has sent me to speak to Sir John."

The Host pointed upstairs and said, "There's his chamber, his house, his castle, his standing-bed and the truckle-bed that can be stored under it. Falstaff's room has been freshly and newly painted with the story of the Prodigal Son. Go knock and call him. May Hell speak like an Anthropophaginian to you. Knock, I say."

An Anthropophaginian is a cannibal, aka man-eater. The Host was joking that Falstaff, if he were irritated by being interrupted, might bite Simple's head off.

"There's an old woman, a fat woman, gone up into Falstaff's bedchamber," Simple said. "I'll be so bold as to stay, sir, until she come down; indeed, I come to speak with her, not him."

"Ha! A fat woman!" the Host said. "The knight may be robbed — I'll call for him."

He shouted, "Bully knight! Bully Sir John! Speak from your lungs military. Are you there? It is your Host, your Ephesian, who is calling for you."

By "Ephesian," the Host meant "jolly companion."

"How are you, my Host?" Falstaff called from upstairs.

"Here's a Bohemian-Tartar who is waiting until the fat woman with you comes down," the Host replied. "Let her descend, bully, let her descend; my chambers are honorable. Do not expect privacy in which to do immoral acts here."

A Bohemian-Tartar is a Tartar from Bohemia — the Host's humorous way of referring to Simple.

Falstaff walked down the stairs and said, "There was, my Host, an old fat woman just now with me; but she's gone."

"Please, sir," Simple said, "wasn't she the wise woman of Brentford?"

A wise woman is a woman who is skilled in occult matters.

"Suppose it was, mussel shell," Falstaff said.

Simple's mouth was habitually open, and his mind was habitually empty; these two characteristics also apply to one mussel shell.

Falstaff continued, "What do you want with her?"

"My master, sir, Master Slender, seeing her walking through the streets, sent me to her to learn, sir, whether one Nym, sir, who cheated him out of a necklace, still had the necklace or not."

"I spoke with the old woman about it," Falstaff said.

"And what did she say, please, sir?"

"She says that the very same man who cheated Master Slender of his chain cozened him of it."

"Cozened" is a word that means "cheated."

"I wish that I could have spoken with the woman herself," Simple said. "I had other things that my master, Master Slender, wanted me to speak to her about."

"What are they?" Falstaff asked. "Let us know."

"Yes," the Host said. "Answer quickly."

"I may not conceal them, sir," Simple replied. He meant "reveal," not "conceal," but the Host joked, "Conceal them, or you die."

"Why, sir, they were only about Miss Anne Page," Simple said. "My master wanted to know if it is his fortune to have her or not."

"It is," Falstaff said. "It is his fortune."

"To what, sir?" Simple asked.

"To have her, or not," Falstaff replied. "Go; tell Slender the fat woman told me that."

"May I be so bold as to say so, sir?" Simple asked.

"Yes, sir," Falstaff said, "as if anyone could be more bold."

"I thank your worship," Simple replied. "I shall make my master glad with these tidings."

Simple exited.

"You are clerkly, you are clerkly, Sir John," the Host replied. "You are a scholar. Was there a wise woman with you?"

"Yes, there was, my Host," Falstaff replied. "She was one who taught me more wit than ever I learned before in my life, and I paid nothing for it neither, but was paid for my learning."

Falstaff was saying that he had learned something from the recent escapade in which he had dressed as a woman. Mr. Ford had paid Falstaff to learn — blows were Falstaff's payment.

Bardolph entered the room and said, "Out, alas, sir! Cozenage, mere cozenage! Cheating, and nothing but cheating!"

Bardolph had ridden with the three Germans who were supposed to be using the Host's horses to ride to the court. He had been riding on a pillion: a cushion behind a saddle for an additional rider.

"Where are my horses?" the Host asked. "Speak well of them, *varletto*."

Varletto was the Host's Italianized word for "varlet." The Host did not want Bardolph to say that the thieves, aka cozeners, had run off with the horses.

"The horses have run away with the cozeners," Bardolph replied. "As soon as we arrived beyond Eton, they threw me off from behind one of them, in a slough of mire; and they used their spurs and rode quickly away, like three German Devils, three Doctor Faustuses."

"They have gone only to meet the Duke, villain," the Host said. "Do not say that they have fled; Germans are honest men."

Sir Hugh entered the room and asked, "Where is the Host?"

"What is the matter, sir?" the Host asked.

"Have a care of your entertainments," Sir Hugh said.

By "entertainments," he meant "those whom you entertain, aka guests in the inn.

Sir Hugh continued, "There is a friend of mine come to town tells me there is three cozen-Germans that has cozened all the hosts of Reading, of Maidenhead, of Colebrook, of horses and money. I tell you for good will, look you: You are wise and full of gibes and vlouting-stocks [flouting-stocks, aka laughing-stocks], and it is not convenient you should be cozened. Fare you well."

"Cozen" meant both "cousin, aka kinsmen or relatives" and "cozening, aka cheating."

Sir Hugh exited the room, and Doctor Caius entered it.

He asked, "Vere [Where] is mine [my] Host de Jarteer [Garter]?"

"Here, Mister Doctor," the Host replied, "in perplexity and doubtful dilemma."

"I cannot tell vat is dat," Doctor Caius said, "but it is tell-a me dat you make grand preparation for a duke de Jamany [from Germany]. By my trot [Truly], dere is no duke dat the court is know to come. I tell you for good vill [will]. *Adieu.*"

He exited.

The Host ordered Bardolph, "Raise the hue and cry, villain, and we will go after the thieves! Assist me, knight. I am undone! Fly, run, hue and cry, villain! I am undone!"

The Host and Bardolph exited.

Falstaff said to himself, "I wish that all the world might be cheated because I have been cheated — and beaten, too. If it should come to the ear of the court how I have been transformed and how my transformation has been washed when I hid in the buck-basket and cudgeled when I disguised myself as a fat woman, they would melt me out of my fat drop by drop and liquor fishermen's boots with me so that the boots would be waterproof. I bet that they would whip me with their fine wits until I were as crest-fallen as a dried pear. I have not prospered ever since I cheated at the card game primero, got caught, and lied about cheating. Well, if my wind were but long enough to say my prayers, I would repent."

Mistress Quickly entered the room.

Falstaff asked, "From where have you come?"

"From the two parties, truly," Mistress Quickly replied.

Of course, she meant that Mrs. Page and Mrs. Ford had sent her to Falstaff.

"The Devil take one party and his dam — his mother — the other!" Falstaff said, "and so they shall be both bestowed. I have suffered more for their sakes, more than the villainous inconstancy of man's disposition — the weakness of man — is able to bear."

"And haven't they suffered?" Mistress Quickly said. "Yes, indeed they have — speciously [Mistress Quickly meant "especially"] one of them. Mrs. Ford, good heart, has been beaten black and blue — you cannot see a white spot on her skin."

"Why are telling you me about black and blue?" Falstaff asked. "I was beaten myself into all the colors of the rainbow; and I was almost arrested as the witch of Brentford. If my admirable dexterity of wit, my counterfeiting the movements of an old woman, had not saved me, the knave constable would have set me in the stocks — in the common stocks — as a witch."

"Sir, let me speak with you in your bedchamber," Mistress Quickly said. "You shall hear how things go; and, I promise you, you will be content. Here is a letter that will help explain things. Good hearts, what trouble it is to bring you together! Surely, one of you has not served Heaven well, or else you would not be so crossed."

"Come up into my bedchamber," Falstaff said.

Fenton and the Host talked together in a room of the Garter Inn.

The Host, who was normally a jovial fellow, was depressed. He said, "Mr. Fenton, don't talk to me; my mind is heavy. I will give up trying to help you marry Anne Page."

"Listen to me for a moment," Fenton said. "Assist me and help me marry Anne Page, and I will give you a hundred pounds in gold more than you lost when the three Germans stole your horses."

"I will listen to you, Mr. Fenton," the Host said, "and I will at the least keep secret what you tell me."

"From time to time I have acquainted you with the dear love I have for fair Anne Page, who has returned my affection as much as she has been allowed to. Her love for me makes me happy. I have a letter from her with such content as will make you wonder. It has mirth that is so intermixed with my desire to marry her that mirth and important matter cannot be separated. Fat Falstaff will take a big role in a great scene: I will reveal to you what that role and scene are — it will be a great jest.

"Listen, my good Host. Tonight at Herne's Oak, between twelve and one o'clock, my sweet Nan is supposed to play the role of the Fairy Queen. The reason why is here in this letter. While she is in this disguise, and while other jests are abundantly going on, her father has commanded her to slip away with Slender and go with him to Eton where they shall be immediately married. She has told her father that she will obey him.

"But, sir, her mother, ever strongly against Slender marrying Miss Anne, and always strongly for Doctor Caius marrying Miss Anne, has arranged that Doctor Caius will spirit her away while other entertainments are keeping everyone busy. There at the deanery, where a priest attends, Doctor Caius is supposed to immediately marry her. Anne has pretended to consent to her mother's plot and has told Doctor Caius that she will marry him.

"This is the way things stand now. Anne's father intends for her to be the only one dressed in white, and at the appropriate time Slender will take her by the hand and tell her to go with him, and they shall leave to be married.

"Anne's mother intends for her to be the only one dressed in green. The colors are important because everyone will be wearing masks and costumes. Doctor Caius will recognize her by the green gown she is wearing. She will also have ribbons hanging from her head and blowing in the wind. At the appropriate time Doctor Caius will pinch her on the hand and tell her to go with him, and they shall leave to be married. Anne has told him that she will go with him."

The Host asked, "Whom does Anne intend to deceive: her father or her mother?"

Fenton replied, "Both, my good Host. She intends to go with me and marry me. And here is what is needed: You will talk to the vicar and have him wait for us at the church between twelve and one. There he shall marry Anne and me to give our hearts united ceremony."

"Well, do your part in the plot properly and husband your resources," the Host said. "I'll go and talk to the vicar. You bring the maiden; you shall not lack a priest."

"I shall evermore be bound to you," Fenton said. "Right now, I will give you some monetary compensation."

CHAPTER 5

— 5.1 —

Falstaff and Mistress Quickly were finishing their conversation.

Falstaff said, "Please, no more prattling; go. I'll keep my promise. This is the third time I have arranged an assignation; I hope good luck lies in odd numbers. Away I go. They say there is divinity in odd numbers, whether in nativity, chance, or death. Away!"

Some people thought that odd numbers were lucky. It was supposed to be good luck to be born or to die or to undertake a venture on an odd-numbered day.

"I will get a chain for you, and I'll do what I can to get you a pair of horns," Mistress Quickly said.

"Away, I say; time is passing," Falstaff said. "Hold up your head, and mince."

He meant for Mistress Quickly to walk away like a lady, with her head held high as she took little steps.

Mistress Quickly exited.

Mr. Ford, in disguise as Mr. Brook, entered Falstaff's room.

Falstaff said, "How are you, Mr. Brook! Mr. Brook, the result of what we have planned will be known tonight, or never. We shall know whether Mr. Ford's wife will commit adultery. Be in the Park about midnight, at Herne's Oak, and you shall see wonders."

"Didn't you visit her yesterday, sir, as you told me you had arranged?"

"I went to her and visited her, Mr. Brook, as you see me, like a poor old man, but I came from her, Mr. Brook, like a poor old woman. Mr. Brook, that same knave Ford, her husband, had the finest mad Devil fit of jealousy in him that ever governed frenzy. I will tell you what happened: He beat me grievously, when I was in the shape of a woman; for when I am in the shape of man, Mr. Brook, I do not even fear Goliath whose spear shaft was as big as a weaver's beam; because I also know that life is a shuttle."

Falstaff had a good knowledge of the Bible.

1 Samuel 17:7 stated, "*And the shaft of his [Goliath's] spear was like a weaver's beam: and his spear head weighed six hundred shekels of iron: and one bearing a shield went before him.*"

Job 7.6 stated, "*My days are swifter than a weaver's shuttle, and they are spent without hope.*"

Falstaff continued, "I am in haste; go along with me. I'll tell you everything, Mr. Brook. Since I plucked geese, played truant, and whipped top, I never knew what it was to be beaten until lately."

Falstaff was saying that he had not been beaten since he was a boy. As a boy, he had done such things as play with tops and pull a feather from a living goose. At school, he had played truant and been whipped for it.

Falstaff continued, "Come with me, and I'll tell you strange things about this knave Ford, on whom tonight I will be revenged, and I will deliver his wife into your hands. Come with me. Strange things are at hand, Mr. Brook! Come with me."

— 5.2 —

At Herne's Oak in Windsor Park, Mr. Page, Justice Shallow, and Slender were talking.

Mr. Page said, "Come, come; we'll lie hidden in the ditch running alongside Windsor Castle until we see the light of our fairies. Remember, son Slender, my daughter —"

Slender interrupted, "Yes, truly. I have spoken with her and we have a password so we can know one another. She will wear white, I will come to her and cry 'mum,' she will reply 'budget,' and so we shall know each other."

A mumbudget is the opposite of a fussbudget. A mumbudget is quiet, while a fussbudget constantly complains.

"That's good, too," Justice Shallow said, "but why do you need either your 'mum' or her 'budget?' She will be the only one wearing white, and so that is enough to know her."

A clock tolled, and Justice Shallow said, "It is ten o'clock."

Mr. Page said, "The night is dark; light and spirits will become it well. May Heaven prosper our sport! No man means evil but the Devil, and we shall know him by his horns. Let's go; follow me."

Mrs. Page, Mrs. Ford, and Doctor Caius talked on a street in Windsor.

Mrs. Page said, "Doctor Caius, my daughter is dressed in green. At the appropriate time, take her by the hand, lead her away to the deanery, and marry her quickly. Go now into the Park. Mrs. Ford and I will go there later, together."

"I know vat [what] I have to do. *Adieu*," Doctor Caius said.

"Fare you well, sir," Mrs. Page said.

Doctor Caius exited.

Mrs. Page continued, "My husband will not rejoice so much at the abuse of Falstaff as he will chafe at the doctor's marrying my daughter, but it does not matter; better a little chiding than a great deal of heartbreak."

Mrs. Ford asked, "Where is Nan now and her troop of fairies, and where is Sir Hugh, who is in costume as a Welsh Devil or evil spirit?"

"They are all lying hidden in a pit near Herne's Oak, with obscured lights. At the moment when Falstaff and we meet, they will immediately uncover their lights."

"That will amaze and frighten him," Mrs. Ford said.

"If he is not frightened, he will be mocked; if he is frightened, he will be mocked even more."

"We'll definitely deceive him," Mrs. Ford said.

"Against such lewdsters and their lechery, those who betray them do no treachery," Mrs. Page said.

"The hour draws on," Mrs. Ford said. "It is almost time! To the oak! To the oak!"

— 5.4 —

Sir Hugh Evans and some others arrived near the oak. Sir Hugh was disguised as a Devil, and the others were disguised as fairies.

"Trib, trib, fairies," Sir Hugh said. "Come; and remember your parts: be pold [bold], please; follow me into the pit; and when I give the watch-'ords [watch-words], do as I pid [bid] you. Come, come; trib, trib."

By "trib," Sir Hugh meant "trip." To move trippingly is to move lightly and quickly.

Falstaff, disguised as Herne the Hunter, stood by himself at Herne's Oak.

He said to himself, "The Windsor bell has struck twelve o'clock; the moment of my meeting with the Windsor wives draws near. Now, may the hot-blooded gods assist me! Remember, Jove, you turned yourself into a bull so you could sleep with Europa; love made you put on your horns. Oh, powerful love! Love, in some respects, makes a beast a man; in some other respects, love makes a man a beast. You also, Jupiter, turned yourself into a swan because of your love of Leda. Oh, omnipotent Love! A swan is not all that different from a goose. How nearly the god acquired the temperament of a silly goose! Jove's fault was done first in the form of a beast. Oh, Jove, a beastly fault! And then another fault in the semblance of a fowl; think about it, Jove; it was a foul — or fowl — fault! When gods have hot backs and lusty loins, what shall poor men do? As for me, I am here in this forest in the form of a horned Windsor stag; and I am the fattest stag, I think, in the forest. Send me a cool rut-time, Jove, or who can blame me if I piss my tallow?"

As a fat man, Falstaff sweat a lot. He was hoping for a cool night in which to perform his lovemaking; that way, he would not excessively sweat. Stags, during rutting time, lose weight as they pursue does with which to mate. People said that the stags lost weight because fat departed their bodies with their urine. Falstaff was worried that he would lose weight through the uncomfortable process of excess sweating and through peeing fat as well as urine.

He heard a noise and said, "Who comes here? My doe?"

Mrs. Ford and Mrs. Page arrived.

Mrs. Ford said, "Sir John! Are you there, my deer? My male deer? My dear?"

"My doe with the black scut!" Falstaff said.

He was being bawdy. A scut is the tail of a deer. Applied to Mrs. Ford, a scut was pubic hair.

Falstaff continued, "Let the sky rain sweet potatoes; let it thunder to the tune of 'Greensleeves,' let it hail kissing-comfits and snow eryngoes — let there come a tempest of provocation and lustful stimulation; I will take shelter here."

Sweet potatoes were thought to be aphrodisiacal, "Greensleeves" was a song about a man whose lady friend was unfaithful to him, kissing-comfits were candies eaten to sweeten the breath, and eryngoes were candied sea holly (also thought to be aphrodisiacal).

The night was dark, so Mrs. Ford said, "Mrs. Page has come with me, sweetheart."

Falstaff, wearing horns like a stag, said, "Divide me like a bribed buck."

He was referring to a stag that had been hunted and killed and now was being cut into pieces and distributed. The buck was a bribed buck because the hunters had bribed a gamekeeper to allow them to hunt the buck.

Falstaff said, "Each of you women will get a haunch."

A haunch is a buttock, useful in the thrusting motion of lovemaking.

He continued, "I will keep my sides for myself, my shoulders for the forester who was bribed, and my horns I bequeath to your husbands. Am I a woodman, ha? Do I speak like Herne the Hunter?"

A woodman was a hunter; what he hunted could be game or women.

Falstaff continued, "Why, Cupid is now a child of conscience; he makes restitution. Twice before I was unsuccessful in my attempts at seduction, but now Cupid will help me succeed! As I am a true spirit, welcome!"

Noises were heard — the "fairies" were shaking their rattles.

Mrs. Page and Mrs. Ford pretended to be frightened.

Mrs. Page said, "What was that?"

Mrs. Ford said, "May Heaven forgive us our sins!"

"What's going on?" Falstaff asked.

Mrs. Page and Mrs. Ford screamed and ran away.

"The Devil must be preventing me from committing adultery and being damned to Hell," Falstaff said. "I think the Devil will not allow me to be damned, lest the oily fat that's in me should set Hell on fire; otherwise, he would not oppose my desire to sin."

Sir Hugh Evans, who was disguised as an evil spirit, and some others disguised as fairies — including one person disguised as the Queen of the Fairies — came out of the pit, carrying lit candles.

The person disguised as the Queen of the Fairies said, "Fairies black, grey, green, and white, you moonshine revelers and shades of night, you orphan heirs of fixed destiny, attend to your duties and your professions.

"Crier Hobgoblin, make the fairy oyes."

Fairies are called orphans because according to tradition they do not have fathers, and they have a fixed destiny because they have duties to perform. The fairy known as Hobgoblin, for example, brings news to the fairies and cries "oyes," which means "Hear ye" or "Listen up."

The person disguised as Hobgoblin said, "Elves, listen for your names; silence, you airy toys. To Windsor chimneys shall leap the fairy named Cricket. If you find fires uncared for and hearths unswept, then pinch the maids as blue as blueberries. Our radiant queen hates bad housekeepers and bad housekeeping."

Falstaff said to himself, "They are fairies; anyone who speaks to them shall die. I'll close my eyes and lie down; no man their works must eye."

He lay down upon his face.

The disguised Sir Hugh said, "Where's Bede? Go you, and where you find a maid who, before she sleeps, has three times her prayers said, cause her to have pleasant dreams; she shall sleep as soundly as a carefree infant. But anyone who sleeps without having prayed for forgiveness of their sins, pinch them — pinch their arms, legs, backs, shoulders, sides, and shins."

The person disguised as the Queen of the Fairies said,

"Go about your business. Search Windsor Castle, elves, within and out. Strew good luck, elves, on every sacred room so that it may stand until the Judgment Day, in a state as wholesome as in state it is fit, worthy the owner, and the owner it.

"The several chairs of order look you scour with juice of balm and every precious flower. Each fair installment, coat, and different crest, with loyal blazon, evermore be blest!"

In the choir of St. George's Chapel in Windsor Castle were 24 stalls, aka places of installment, each devoted to one of the 24 Knights of the Garter. Fixed to the back of each stall was a coat of arms, and on top of each stall was the knight's helmet and the particular heraldic device that decorated that particular knight's helmet.

The person disguised as the Queen of the Fairies continued, "And nightly, meadow-fairies, look you sing, similar to the Garter's circle, in a ring."

The emblem of the Order of the Garter is a blue ribbon that forms a circle as it is worn above the knee. A garter is a narrow band of clothing that is fastened on the leg and used to keep up stockings.

The person disguised as the Queen of the Fairies continued, "The appearance of the fairy ring pressed on the ground, green let it be, more fertile-fresh than all the field to see."

Fairy rings are circles on the ground that are a darker green than the other grass.

The person disguised as the Queen of the Fairies continued, "And *Honi soit qui mal y pense* write in emerald branches and flowers purple, blue, and white. Let sapphire, pearl, and rich embroidery be buckled below fair knighthood's bending knee. Fairies use flowers for their writing."

Honi soit qui mal y pense is French for "Shame to him who thinks evil." This is the motto of the Most Noble Order of the Garter, which was founded in 1348 by King Edward III. He picked up a lady's garter that had accidentally fallen on the floor. Other people saw him and laughed, and he said the French words that became the motto of the order.

The person disguised as the Queen of the Fairies continued, "Away; disperse — but until one o'clock we must dance our dance of custom round about the Oak of Herne the Hunter. Let us not forget."

The disguised Sir Hugh said, "Please, lock hand in hand; yourselves in order set and twenty glow-worms shall our lanterns be, to guide our measure — our dance — round about the tree. But, wait! I smell a man of middle-earth."

A man of middle-earth is a mortal male human being. Middle-earth is located between Heaven and Hell.

The "fairies" discovered Falstaff, who said to himself, "Heavens defend me from that Welsh fairy, lest he transform me to a piece of cheese!"

Sir Hugh retained some of his Welsh accent despite making an effort to speak without it. Falstaff, despite being frightened by the fairies, was joking about the stereotype of cheese-loving Welsh people.

The person disguised as Hobgoblin said to Falstaff, "Vile worm, you were looked over and bewitched by the evil eye even during your birth."

The person disguised as the Queen of the Fairies said, "With trial-fire touch his finger's end. If he be chaste, the flame will back descend and cause no pain; but if he reacts with pain, his is the flesh of a corrupted heart."

The person disguised as Hobgoblin said, "Let us have a trial by fire."

The disguised Sir Hugh said, "Let us see if this wood will catch fire."

Sir Hugh burned Falstaff's fingers with his candle.

Falstaff said, "Ouch! Ouch! Ouch!"

The person disguised as the Queen of the Fairies said, "He is corrupt — corrupt, and tainted in desire! Go around him, fairies; sing a scornful rhyme; and, as you trip, pinch him in time with your song."

The "fairies" sang this song:

"Down with sinful fantasy!

"Down with lust and lechery!

"Lust is but a fire in the blood,

"Kindled with unchaste desire,

"Fed in heart, whose flames aspire

"As thoughts do blow them, higher and higher.

"Pinch him, all you fairies, painfully;

"Pinch him for his villainy;

"Pinch him, and burn him, and turn him about,

"Until candles and starlight and moonshine be out."

As the "fairies" danced around Falstaff and pinched him, Doctor Caius arrived and led away a "fairy" wearing green, and Slender arrived and led away a "fairy" wearing white. Then Fenton arrived. Anne Page — who was also disguised as a fairy — went to him, and they ran away together. In the midst of all this activity, hunting horns sounded and the other "fairies" ran away a short distance. Falstaff stood up.

Mrs. Ford and Mrs. Page, pursued by Mr. Ford and Mr. Page, ran over to Falstaff.

Feigning anger, Mr. Page said to his wife, "No, do not run away from me. I have watched you and caught you in the act. Will no one but Herne the Hunter do for you?"

Mrs. Page replied, "Please, let's end this jest now."

She then said, "Now, good Sir John, how do you like the wives of Windsor?"

She added, "Do you see these horns on his head, husband? Aren't these fair yokes better in the forest than in the town?"

Mr. Ford asked Falstaff, "Now, sir, who's a cuckold now?"

He showed Falstaff the beard that he had used to disguise himself as Mr. Brook, and then he mimicked Falstaff's overuse of the two words "Mr. Brook": "Mr. Brook, Falstaff's a knave, a cuckoldly knave. Here are his horns, Mr. Brook: and, Mr. Brook, he has enjoyed nothing of Ford's but his buck-basket, his cudgel, and twenty pounds of money, which must be paid back to Mr. Brook. His horses have been legally seized until the money is paid back, Mr. Brook."

Mrs. Ford said, "Sir John, we have had ill luck; we could never meet and do anything naughty. I will never take you for my love again, but I will always regard you as my deer."

"I do begin to perceive that I am made an ass," Falstaff said.

"True, and an ox too," Mr. Ford said. "Both the proofs are evident."

Falstaff had been made an ass — a fool. He had also — in a way — been made an ox, aka cuckold, as shown by the horns he was wearing. The women he wanted to sleep with were sleeping with other men — their husbands.

"These are not fairies," Falstaff said, looking at some of the children who had pretended to be fairies. "Three or four times I thought they were not fairies, and yet the guiltiness of my mind and the sudden ambush of my wits drove the obviousness of the trickery into a genuine belief — in the teeth of all rhyme and reason — that they were fairies. See now how intelligence may be made a Jack-a-Lent — a puppet for children to throw things at during Lent — when intelligence is used for ill purposes!"

Sir Hugh, who had resumed his heavy Welsh accent now that he was no longer playing a role, said, "Sir John Falstaff, serve Got [God], and leave your desires, and fairies will not pinse [pinch] you."

"Well said, fairy Hugh," Falstaff replied.

Sir Hugh said to Mr. Ford, "And leave your jealousies, too, please."

Mr. Ford replied, "I will never mistrust my wife again until you are able to woo her while using good English."

Falstaff said, "Have I laid my brain in the Sun and dried it, so that it lacks intelligence to prevent so gross overreaching as this? Am I ridden with a Welsh goat, too? Shall I have a coxcomb of frieze — a fool's hat made from Welsh woolen fabric? It is time I were choked with a piece of toasted cheese."

Sir Hugh said, "Seese [Cheese] is not good to give putter [butter]; your belly is all putter."

He meant that it was not healthy for Falstaff to put cheese in his belly because his belly was made of butter — butter creates a fat belly — and it is not healthy to eat too much butter and too much cheese.

"'Seese' and 'putter'!" Falstaff said. "Have I lived to stand and be taunted by one who makes fritters of English?"

Fritters are fried pieces of dough. Inside the dough are pieces of chopped-up foods such as meat or fruit.

Falstaff continued, "This is enough to be the decay of lust and late-walking for immoral purposes through the realm."

"Why, Sir John," Mrs. Page asked, "do you think that even if we would have thrust the virtue out of our hearts by the head and shoulders and have given ourselves without scruple to Hell, that the Devil ever could have made *you* our delight?"

Mr. Ford asked, "Could *you* be their delight? Could they delight in a sausage made out of numerous ingredients? Could they delight in a bulky bag of flax?"

Mrs. Page asked, "Could we delight in a puffed-up fat man?"

Mr. Page asked, "Could they delight in an old, cold, withered man who is made of intolerable fat guts."

Mr. Ford asked, "Could they delight in a man who is as slanderous as Satan?"

Mr. Page asked, "Could they delight in a man who is as poor as Job?"

Mr. Ford asked, "Could they delight in a man who is as wicked as Job's wife?"

Sir Hugh asked, "Could they delight in a man who is given to fornications, and to taverns and sack and wine and metheglins [spiced Welsh mead], and to drinkings and swearings and starings, pribbles and prabbles [bribbles, aka quibbles, and brabbles, aka trivial disputes]?"

"Well, I am the theme of your mockery," Falstaff said. "You have the better of me; I am dejected; I am not able to answer the Welsh flannel who is Sir Hugh. Ignorance itself is a plummet over me. I have been so ignorant that ignorance itself is less ignorant than I am. Therefore, treat me as you will."

Mr. Ford said, "Indeed, sir, we'll bring you to Windsor, to one Mr. Brook, whom you have cheated of money, to whom you would have been a pander.

Over and above what you have already suffered, I think to repay that money will be a biting affliction to you."

Mr. Page added, "Yet be cheerful, knight. You shall eat a posset tonight at my house."

A posset is a drink to be drunk and is not normally regarded as a food to be eaten; however, a posset can be regarded as a food for invalids.

Mr. Page added, "In my home I will want you to laugh at my wife, who now is laughing at you. Tell her that Mr. Slender has married her daughter."

Mrs. Page thought, *Doctors doubt that. If Anne Page is my daughter, she is, by this time, Doctor Caius' wife.*

"Doctors doubt that" meant "scholars disagree." Of course, Mrs. Page thought that Doctor Caius would doubt that Anne Page had married Slender since by this time he — Doctor Caius — should have married Anne Page.

Slender walked up to the group and said, "Hey, father Page!"

By "father," he meant "father-in-law," but that was not an accurate title.

My. Page said, "Son, hello! Hello, son! Have you completed the business you wanted to complete tonight?"

By "son," he meant "son-in-law," but that was not an accurate title.

Slender said, "Completed the business! I'll make the best people in Gloucestershire know what has happened about that business. I wish that I would be hanged if I do not."

"What has happened about that business, son?" Mr. Page asked. He was referring to the business of Slender marrying Mr. Page's daughter, Anne Page.

Slender replied, "I went yonder to the village of Eton to marry Miss Anne Page, and I found out that the person I thought was Miss Anne Page was actually a big clumsy boy. If we had not been in the church, I would have beaten him, or he would have beaten me. If I did not think it had been Anne Page, I wish I would go to sleep and never wake up again! I thought it was Anne Page, and here it was a postmaster's boy!"

The postmaster was in charge of post horses — horses that could be ridden from one town to another for a fee. The postmaster's boy — servant — helped take care of the horses.

"Upon my life, then, you took the wrong fairy," Mr. Page said.

"You don't need to tell me that," Slender said. "I do in fact think that I took the wrong fairy; after all, I took a boy and not a girl. I swear that if I had been married to him, I would not have had him even though he was wearing women's apparel."

Mr. Page said, "Why, this is your own folly. Didn't I tell you how you should know my daughter — by the color of her garments?"

Slender replied, "I went to the 'fairy' wearing white, and I said, 'Mum,' and 'she' said, 'Budget,' as Anne and I had arranged; and yet it was not Anne, but a postmaster's boy."

Mrs. Page said, "Good George, do not be angry. I knew about your plan to have Slender marry Anne, and so I had my daughter dress in green; and, indeed, she is now with Doctor Caius at the deanery, and there they have been married."

Doctors doubt that.

Doctor Caius now arrived and said, "Vere [Where] is Miss Page? By gar [God], I am cozened [cheated]! I ha' [have] married *un garcon*, a boy; *un paysan* [peasant], by gar, a boy! It is not Anne Page! By gar, I am cozened!"

Mrs. Page asked, "Didn't you run away with the 'fairy' wearing green?"

"Yes, by gar, and it is a boy," Doctor Caius said. "By gar, I'll wake up everybody in Windsor."

He exited.

"This is strange," Mr. Ford said. "Who has gotten the right Anne?"

"My heart troubles me," Mr. Page said. "Look. Here comes Mr. Fenton."

Fenton and Anne Page walked up to the group.

Mr. Page said, "Hello, Mr. Fenton."

"Pardon me, good father!" Anne Page said. "My good mother, pardon me!"

Mr. Page asked, "How did it happen that you did not go with Mr. Slender?"

Mrs. Page asked, "How did it happen that you did not go with Doctor Caius?"

Fenton replied for Anne Page: "You are overwhelming her. Hear the truth about what happened. You would have married her most shamefully; in the marriages you proposed for her there was no love. The truth is that she and I have been in love for a long time and have been engaged to marry each other. We are now entirely sure that nothing can dissolve the union between us because we are legally married. The offence that she has committed is holy. Her deceit cannot be called crafty, disobedient, or unduteous because by marrying me she has avoided and shunned the thousand irreligious cursed hours that a forced and loveless marriage would have brought upon her."

Mr. Ford said to the Pages, "Do not stand here shocked. What's done is done. When it comes to love, the Heavens themselves do rule. Money buys land, but not wives, who are acquired through the workings of fate."

Falstaff said, "I am glad that although you took a special stand to strike at me, your arrow has glanced off me. I am not the only one wounded tonight."

Mr. Page said, "Well, what can I do? Fenton, may Heaven give you joy! What cannot be avoided must be embraced."

Falstaff observed, "When dogs run at night, all sorts of deer are chased."

Mrs. Page said, "Well, I will grumble no further. Mr. Fenton, may Heaven give you many, many merry days!"

She added, "Good husband, let all of us — including Sir John — go to our home, and laugh at tonight's doings over a country fire."

"Good idea," Mr. Ford said.

He added, "Sir John, to Mr. Brook you yet shall keep your word for he tonight shall lie with Mrs. Ford."

APPENDIX A: ABOUT THE AUTHOR

It was a dark and stormy night. Suddenly a cry rang out, and on a hot summer night in 1954, Josephine, wife of Carl Bruce, gave birth to a boy — me. Unfortunately, this young married couple allowed Reuben Saturday, Josephine's brother, to name their first-born. Reuben, aka "The Joker," decided that Bruce was a nice name, so he decided to name me Bruce Bruce. I have gone by my middle name — David — ever since.

Being named Bruce David Bruce hasn't been all bad. Bank tellers remember me very quickly, so I don't often have to show an ID. It can be fun in charades, also. When I was a counselor as a teenager at Camp Echoing Hills in Warsaw, Ohio, a fellow counselor gave the signs for "sounds like" and "two words," then she pointed to a bruise on her leg twice. Bruise Bruise? Oh yeah, Bruce Bruce is the answer!

Uncle Reuben, by the way, gave me a haircut when I was in kindergarten. He cut my hair short and shaved a small bald spot on the back of my head. My mother wouldn't let me go to school until the bald spot grew out again.

Of all my brothers and sisters (six in all), I am the only transplant to Athens, Ohio. I was born in Newark, Ohio, and have lived all around Southeastern Ohio. However, I moved to Athens to go to Ohio University and have never left.

At Ohio U, I never could make up my mind whether to major in English or Philosophy, so I got a bachelor's degree with a double major in both areas, then I added a master's degree in English and a master's degree in Philosophy. Yes, I have my MAMA degree.

Currently, and for a long time to come (I eat fruits and veggies), I am spending my retirement writing books such as *Nadia Comaneci: Perfect 10*, *The Funniest People in Dance*, *Homer's* Iliad: *A Retelling in Prose*, and *William Shakespeare's* Othello: *A Retelling in Prose*.

By the way, my sister Brenda Kennedy writes romances such as *A New Beginning* and *Shattered Dreams*.

APPENDIX B: SOME BOOKS BY DAVID BRUCE

Retellings of a Classic Work of Literature

Arden of Faversham: *A Retelling*

Ben Jonson's The Alchemist: *A Retelling*

Ben Jonson's The Arraignment, or Poetaster: *A Retelling*

Ben Jonson's Bartholomew Fair: *A Retelling*

Ben Jonson's The Case is Altered: *A Retelling*

Ben Jonson's Catiline's Conspiracy: *A Retelling*

Ben Jonson's The Devil is an Ass: *A Retelling*

Ben Jonson's Epicene: *A Retelling*

Ben Jonson's Every Man in His Humor: *A Retelling*

Ben Jonson's Every Man Out of His Humor: *A Retelling*

Ben Jonson's The Fountain of Self-Love, or Cynthia's Revels: *A Retelling*

Ben Jonson's The Magnetic Lady, or Humors Reconciled: *A Retelling*

Ben Jonson's The New Inn, or The Light Heart: *A Retelling*

Ben Jonson's Sejanus' Fall: *A Retelling*

Ben Jonson's The Staple of News: *A Retelling*

Ben Jonson's A Tale of a Tub: *A Retelling*

Ben Jonson's Volpone, or the Fox: *A Retelling*

Christopher Marlowe's Complete Plays: Retellings

Christopher Marlowe's Dido, Queen of Carthage: *A Retelling*

Christopher Marlowe's Doctor Faustus: *Retellings of the 1604 A-Text and of the 1616 B-Text*

Christopher Marlowe's Edward II: *A Retelling*

Christopher Marlowe's The Massacre at Paris: *A Retelling*

Christopher Marlowe's The Rich Jew of Malta: *A Retelling*

Christopher Marlowe's Tamburlaine, Parts 1 and 2: *Retellings*

Dante's Divine Comedy: *A Retelling in Prose*

Dante's Inferno: *A Retelling in Prose*

Dante's Purgatory: *A Retelling in Prose*

Dante's Paradise: *A Retelling in Prose*

The Famous Victories of Henry V: *A Retelling*

From the Iliad *to the* Odyssey: *A Retelling in Prose of Quintus of Smyrna's* Posthomerica

George Chapman, Ben Jonson, and John Marston's Eastward Ho! *A Retelling*

George Peele's The Arraignment of Paris: *A Retelling*

George Peele's The Battle of Alcazar: *A Retelling*

George's Peele's David and Bathsheba, and the Tragedy of Absalom: *A Retelling*

George Peele's Edward I: *A Retelling*

George Peele's The Old Wives' Tale: *A Retelling*

William Shakespeare's 38 Plays: Retellings in Prose
William Shakespeare's 1 Henry IV, aka Henry IV, Part 1: *A Retelling in Prose*
William Shakespeare's 2 Henry IV, aka Henry IV, Part 2: *A Retelling in Prose*
William Shakespeare's 1 Henry VI, aka Henry VI, Part 1: *A Retelling in Prose*
William Shakespeare's 2 Henry VI, aka Henry VI, Part 2: *A Retelling in Prose*
William Shakespeare's 3 Henry VI, aka Henry VI, Part 3: *A Retelling in Prose*
William Shakespeare's All's Well that Ends Well: *A Retelling in Prose*
William Shakespeare's Antony and Cleopatra: *A Retelling in Prose*
William Shakespeare's As You Like It: *A Retelling in Prose*
William Shakespeare's The Comedy of Errors: *A Retelling in Prose*
William Shakespeare's Coriolanus: *A Retelling in Prose*
William Shakespeare's Cymbeline: *A Retelling in Prose*
William Shakespeare's Hamlet: *A Retelling in Prose*
William Shakespeare's Henry V: *A Retelling in Prose*
William Shakespeare's Henry VIII: *A Retelling in Prose*
William Shakespeare's Julius Caesar: *A Retelling in Prose*
William Shakespeare's King John: *A Retelling in Prose*
William Shakespeare's King Lear: *A Retelling in Prose*
William Shakespeare's Love's Labor's Lost: *A Retelling in Prose*
William Shakespeare's Macbeth: *A Retelling in Prose*
William Shakespeare's Measure for Measure: *A Retelling in Prose*
William Shakespeare's The Merchant of Venice: *A Retelling in Prose*
William Shakespeare's The Merry Wives of Windsor: *A Retelling in Prose*
William Shakespeare's A Midsummer Night's Dream: *A Retelling in Prose*
William Shakespeare's Much Ado About Nothing: *A Retelling in Prose*
William Shakespeare's Othello: *A Retelling in Prose*
William Shakespeare's Pericles, Prince of Tyre: *A Retelling in Prose*
William Shakespeare's Richard II: *A Retelling in Prose*
William Shakespeare's Richard III: *A Retelling in Prose*
William Shakespeare's Romeo and Juliet: *A Retelling in Prose*
William Shakespeare's The Taming of the Shrew: *A Retelling in Prose*
William Shakespeare's The Tempest: *A Retelling in Prose*
William Shakespeare's Timon of Athens: *A Retelling in Prose*
William Shakespeare's Titus Andronicus: *A Retelling in Prose*
William Shakespeare's Troilus and Cressida: *A Retelling in Prose*
William Shakespeare's Twelfth Night: *A Retelling in Prose*
William Shakespeare's The Two Gentlemen of Verona: *A Retelling in Prose*
William Shakespeare's The Two Noble Kinsmen: *A Retelling in Prose*
William Shakespeare's The Winter's Tale: *A Retelling in Prose*